WHAT SHE KNEW

Regan Black

A Novel

CHAPTER ONE

Sunday October 14

Her house of cards was swaying. About to topple.

Dr. Luciana Perez sat in her home office, her chair turned toward the gray, rainy evening on the other side of the window. The vibrant fall color of the trees behind her house had been muted by the weather as well as her mood. On the desk, her cell phone chimed with yet another text message alert and she ignored it, her courage momentarily failing her.

She'd heard the news via text an hour ago and she had yet to shake off the chill that washed over her. A young woman, stripped to the waist, had been pulled from the river. The body was not immediately recognizable, thanks to the natural course of decomposition, but she could almost hear the name in the ping and patter of raindrops against the glass: *Josie Rodriguez.*

Ana had never been more grateful that her scope of work at the Shutter Lake Medical Clinic didn't include serving as the coroner.

The text message notifying her about the body had been from

her friend Dana Perkins. Dana, a superb psychologist and principal of Shutter Lake School, had been worried about Josie for weeks. Ana knew this wasn't the answer Dana had hoped for when she asked their friend Julia Ford, a former investigative reporter to look into the girl's disappearance.

Maybe it wasn't Josie after all.

If only. A bitter, half-sob slipped through Ana's lips. If the remains turned out to be someone other than Josie, the tension and fear gripping Shutter Lake would only increase exponentially. She had a few patients who didn't need that kind of stress exacerbating underlying concerns and conditions.

Some of the brightest minds in industry, technology, and banking had come together to build and develop this town, planting their idea of paradise in the gorgeous Sierra Mountains of northern California. From the school to the cutting edge medical clinic she ran to the commitment to the arts, Shutter Lake had been a slice of heaven. More than a home, here she'd found the peace and stability she needed to heal even as she engaged her skills to heal others.

She loved being their doctor, caring for the community as a whole. Her staff, carefully selected, had become a second family and a high-functioning team every bit as essential to delivering excellent care as the state-of-the-art equipment the city council provided.

Murder had changed that.

A familiar voice in her head urged her to run. Now, before she became the next victim.

Now. Quickly. Tonight.

But where could she possibly go?

At forty, with years of experience in private practice, her resume should stand on its own. But what if her next employer picked away the thin veneer hiding her past like old polish chipping off a fingernail? The world was becoming smaller every day and previously buried secrets were up for grabs. Sylvia Cole's murder was all the encouragement Ana needed to tread lightly.

This position had been the equivalent of a lightning strike, the right opportunity opening up at the perfect time. The seamless combination of the well-equipped clinic, the stunning house, and the reliable support of a city council focused on encouraging healthy lifestyle choices was so rare as to be almost mythical. She'd been a fool to assume it could last forever.

As Dr. Perez, she'd often been praised for her medical brilliance and compassion with patients, but she'd done herself a great disservice by allowing her escape hatch to rust over. She rested her head against the cool window glass. After everything, it was hard to accept that complacency in the midst of a compassionate effort would be her undoing.

Seeking to calm her skittering nerves, she told herself it was only a problem if she survived the current crisis. Assuming the person who'd murdered Sylvia was also responsible for the disappearances of Josie and a missing FBI agent. If that person managed to kill her next, she wouldn't be in a position to care what skeletons spilled from her closet.

She closed her eyes, well aware that she wasn't ready to give up, give in, or die. Where did that leave her? Alive or dead, she couldn't see a way that this situation ended well for her. That meant it was time to get proactive about either telling the truth or escaping Shutter Lake.

Her phone chimed again, twice. Someone needed her attention, needed her to put her own worries aside. Reminding herself she'd overcome enormous obstacles to reach this respected status in a community that cared for her as much as she cared for it, she rallied and picked up her phone.

Not the clinic. The message had come through in two parts from the deputy chief of police, Laney Holt. She was requesting an emergency girls' night out. The second text specified the Wine and Cheese House and a later than usual time due to the circumstances of finding a body in the river.

Having three girls' nights in one week was unprecedented. Clearly, times had changed in Shutter Lake.

A third message popped up from Julia. She and Dana would get a table and Ana and Laney were expected to arrive as soon as possible. Ana sent a quick confirmation.

Barring an emergency, Ana had no excuse to avoid the gathering. Deep down, the wounded girl she'd been warred with the woman she'd become. This wasn't the time to give in to old fears. Laney, the only member of the Shutter Lake PD with experience investigating murder, had been diligently working to find Sylvia's killer. If she could overcome the trauma that drove her to leave a good career as a detective with the Los Angeles PD, Ana could pull herself together and be supportive.

Here in Shutter Lake, she'd learned that's what friends did. Support, listen, nurture. Friends had been a rare commodity in Ana's life and it still surprised her that she had four—no, three. Sylvia was dead. God, she missed her. Her heart felt sluggish whenever Sylvia came to mind and these days, with a murderer on the loose, it was impossible to think of anything else.

The younger woman had been born and raised here and grown into a vibrant, vital part of the community. And she'd gone out of her way to welcome Ana. They'd bonded over their mutually fierce independence and love of chocolate. In Sylvia, she'd found a confidant she'd never dared to hope for.

Still, to have three women in that treasured category of friendship was a big accomplishment considering where she'd started.

Naturally the discovery of a second body, another young woman, would affect everyone in town as the news spread. Shutter Lake had been shocked when Sylvia, a respected entrepreneur, creator and owner of Sparkle cleaning service, was found murdered in her home. Sylvia's parents were devastated and her father kept upping the reward for any information leading to justice for his daughter.

But Ana's friends would be taking this discovery harder than most in town, for vastly different reasons. All four of them had settled in Shutter Lake, choosing lucrative, lower-stress jobs that allowed them to hide and heal from tragedy-laden pasts.

Laney had found a measure of peace in the slower pace of Shutter Lake after devastating events during the case that was her last with the LAPD. Dana arrived eager to move forward and determined to serve faculty and students here after losing four of her Kindergarten students during a school shooting in Phoenix. Julia still dealt with lingering panic and aftershocks, especially this time of year. While following a story on the Jack o' Lantern serial killer of Chicago, she'd been kidnapped by the monster and only escaped by killing him.

As their primary physician, Ana was privy to how those dreadful events impacted her patients. Having personally escaped a vicious start in life, she knew firsthand how the old memories could crop up and interfere at the most inopportune times.

They all worked daily to stay ahead of the ghosts haunting them. Having friends to be open with cast a light into the shadows, dispelling those ghosts.

Tell them.

Her breath stuttered in and out of her lungs and she quickly dismissed the thought. There were some things friends couldn't change. Some secrets that, once shared, would only backfire and hurt everyone.

Sylvia's murder was proof enough of that. She'd done more than keep her clients' homes clean. She'd observed and discovered secrets ranging from curious to problematic. As far as Ana knew Sylvia had never once broadcast those secrets. Still, it was likely someone had killed her to keep her quiet. Although Ana had a vague notion about the killer's identity, she didn't have evidence to back up her theory. Laney needed more than speculation to close out this investigation.

Swallowing her anguish over losing a dear friend, Ana deliberately shifted her thinking toward her analytical side. Yolanda Cole, Sylvia's mother was suffering from increasing grief and stress issues. In the days since her daughter's body had been found she'd been to the clinic twice —once for chest pains and once for sleeplessness. Ana made a mental note to ask Laney tonight when the police intended to release Sylvia's body. Yolanda and Zion needed the emotional closure despite the ongoing investigation.

Her lower lip trembled and she caught it between her teeth. Tears blurred her vision much like the rain blurred the view outside her window. She'd cried over Sylvia, privately, and would likely do so again. But not now when swollen, red-rimmed eyes would only bring unwanted attention from her friends. With everything they were dealing with, her personal grief was the least of their trouble.

Any minute now, Ana would be strong enough, clear-eyed enough to drive back into town, passing by Sylvia's house still marred with crime scene tape, to meet her friends.

She took a deep breath. And another. Striding out of her office, she paused in the hall bath and brushed her hair, pulling it back into a sleek ponytail, dabbing a little gloss onto her lips. At the hall tree by the front door, she dropped her phone into her purse and unhooked her keys from the leather tab that held them. Staying organized kept her calm. That calm had carried her through the highs and lows of remaking her life.

Setting her alarm system and activating the cameras inside and out, she headed for her car. Her cell phone hummed with a message just before she turned from her drive to Olive Tree Lane. A little ashamed that she hoped it was an emergency, she braked and grabbed the phone to check.

The text message was from Dana, suggesting she hurry if she wanted any of the stuffed mushrooms. Amused, Ana felt her lips curl and her heart lift. Leave it to Dana to say just the right thing, whether she knew it or not. The woman had a gift and it was a pleasure to coordinate with such a talented professional when a patient needed both of them.

When Ana reached the restaurant, decorated with the seasonal golds and ambers of fall, she was steadier and grateful for it. The three women had a glass of her favorite wine waiting for her as she slid into the booth to join them. Yes, friends were a treasure.

She looked at each of them in turn, soaking up the glow of happiness that she'd found a place to belong. Even if it couldn't last, she wouldn't toss away such a rare joy in the midst of an emotion-ridden crisis. Changing names to protect the innocent didn't make her any less their friend.

"You okay?" Dana asked.

"Great," she lied smoothly.

Julia nudged the plate with one lone stuffed mushroom closer to her. "Long day?"

"Not as long as yours," Ana replied. She was pleased to see they'd all taken the time to change into warm, dry clothing before coming back out tonight. None of them were showing typical cold symptoms, but if she could make it easier on them she would.

She patted her purse. "I stopped by the clinic and picked up some cold medicine samples. It wasn't the best day to be outside for hours on end." Taking care of the physical was only one part of the equation in her mind.

"You can take the doctor out of the clinic," Laney said with a wry chuckle. "Can't take the clinic out of the doc."

"We're all happy to be alive enough to catch a cold," Julia murmured into her wine. "Poor Josie."

Laney shot her a quelling glance. "We don't have an ID on the victim yet."

Though the odds of them being overheard were low, Ana appreciated Laney's caution.

"She'd clearly been in the water a while," Julia said with a small shudder.

"Which makes identification more challenging," Laney reminded her in low tones.

Ana kept her professional mask in place to hide her revulsion at the images that comment evoked. As the primary physician for an entire town, she'd quickly learned to hide any inkling of judgment over anything her patients divulged. Laney had proven equally circumspect with information regarding the investigation.

"Hopefully we'll know something before the press conference tomorrow," Laney continued.

"Usual time?" Julia asked.

"And the usual place," Laney confirmed.

All of the press conferences since Sylvia's death had been held in front of City Hall on Monday evenings at five o'clock. Based on what Ana was seeing with her patients, she wasn't sure the gatherings were reassuring the community as much as the police department and city council hoped.

Laney raised her wine glass to her lips. With her blond hair pulled back into a ponytail, her unframed face appeared far too young for the horrors she'd seen along the way.

"I really wish I could have identified her," Dana murmured, staring into her wine.

Ana exchanged a knowing look with Laney as she patted Dana's shoulder. "The officials will handle it. Soon, I'm sure."

"Laney didn't let me close enough," Dana continued. "I get it," she added, summoning a weak smile for the deputy chief. "I just wanted to spare the Windermeres."

In their sixties, Katherine and Quentin Windermere had been instrumental in founding the town. They'd never had children of their own so they hosted exchange students every semester. Josie Rodriguez had stayed with them for a short time, diving into the community so deeply she even took a part-time job with Sparkle. Then one day, she was simply gone. Katherine had called the school to inform Dana well after the fact, explaining Josie would be absent because she'd returned to Venezuela for a family emergency.

"Her mother's nearby," Julia said to Dana. "And I'm sure there's DNA somewhere between her room at the Windermere's or even Sparkle. Right Laney?"

"You know I can't discuss any details of the investigation," Laney said.

"Right. You also know we're here because *you* asked us to come. Between the four of us we're practically a brain trust," Dana reminded her. "Four heads are better than one and you need a solid lead."

"True," Laney allowed. She looked directly at Ana. "You knew Sylvia better than we did. Any thoughts on who wanted her dead?"

Tell them.

Sylvia had never joined them for girls' night, despite Ana's invitations and encouragement. Respecting that, she shook her head. "No one has confessed," she replied. "Unless you're asking about a specific patient, suspected of criminal behavior, confidentiality is still binding."

Laney only pursed her lips.

"In my professional opinion," Ana continued, "Sylvia was not disposed to violence." Ana rolled her shoulders. "As her friend, I can assure you she never told me she wanted to toss anyone in a river, much less an employee she delighted in. Assuming the remains belong to Josie."

"I'm not attacking you, Ana," Laney said, her voice cool. "Just looking for insight."

Ana supposed between them, she and Dana and Laney knew most of Shutter Lake's secrets. People tended to trust the three of them. If only Sylvia's killer would confide in one of them, by accident or design, they might make some progress.

"I understand." Ana stayed calm as three pairs of eyes studied her. "This is difficult for all of us." She sipped her wine. "What made you go down to the river?" Ana asked Julia.

"Dana," Julia replied. "You know she asked me to dust off my investigative reporting skills and dig into Josie's disappearance."

Ana nodded. Nothing mattered to Dana as much as the safety and welfare of her students.

"So you could focus on Sylvia," Dana said to Laney.

"I was never offended," Laney replied with a warm, confident smile.

It was a lovely expression that nurtured trust and defused tension whether Laney was taking a statement on a missing dog or dealing with a fender bender. Until Sylvia's murder that had been the worst of crimes to cope with in Shutter Lake.

Unfortunately, it was not the expression Laney aimed Ana's way tonight. She couldn't decipher what her friend was thinking, only the unsettling reaction it created. Had the investigation turned up something—past or present—that pointed to Ana as a suspect?

Run.

She wanted to rip that voice out of her head. Fear, panic, or knee-jerk reactions never solved anything.

"Ana?" Julia tapped her fingernail on the table.

She blinked rapidly, clearing away the cobwebs of her past. "Yes, sorry. You were saying?"

"A witness remembered seeing a man standing alone on the Mill River bridge, staring at the water a few weeks back," Julia explained.

"She couldn't pin down the exact date and she didn't have much of a description since it was late at night, but like you with the cold meds, we followed intuition and went to look around."

"Are you all right?" Ana's question was for all of them.

"Finding that shoe tangled in the brush didn't leave me much hope for a positive outcome," Julia admitted. "I wanted so badly to be wrong and have you three accuse me of turning back into a cynical reporter."

The laughter around the table was brittle and brief.

"I can't imagine the shock of it," Ana said. Except she could, having faced the grim finality of death before her twelfth birthday, long before her studies in medical school.

Julia twisted her wineglass side to side, watching the golden liquid roll and glide. "Now we just need to find Special Agent Adler."

"The hunk's missing partner?" she asked, trying to make Julia smile.

It almost worked. Julia's old flame, Special Agent Patrick Richards had come to town less than a week ago on the trail of his partner Evan Adler who seemed to have disappeared. Julia had adamantly sworn off rekindling any romance with Rick but Ana recognized the telltale signs of Julia struggling with old memories. The fall season troubled her enough without having her ex around.

When asked, she'd told Julia she hadn't seen Adler. It wasn't a lie, but it wasn't the full truth either. Sylvia had mentioned the FBI agent was coming to town to visit with her about Josie's disappearance. Ana's stomach twisted. Recognizing the signs of anxiety, she once again coached herself away from the abyss of full disclosure.

If she blurted out everything right now, she wouldn't be able to help people who needed her still. Patients like Yolanda, wrecked by grief, and Troy Duval who was dealing with the progression of his Multiple Sclerosis.

Better to wait for the facts to come in. If the girl from the river wasn't Josie, Ana would have exposed herself to persecution—and worse—for no reason.

"If the girl you found is Josie, why would the Windermeres cover up her disappearance?" Ana queried.

"They didn't know," Julia said. "They believed the family emergency thing. Quentin saw her through security. Then poof." She flicked her fingers.

Ana had her doubts. She met Laney's gaze. "What about her family?"

"Her parents came up to Grass Valley when she got the exchange student spot," Laney said. "After so much time without any word, they'd gone to the local police to list her as missing."

"Naturally, they haven't looked too hard," Julia muttered. "Lumping her in with the typical angst-ridden teenagers who turn into runaways. Her mother recently met with Mr. and Mrs. Windermere too, begging for help to find her."

Josie hadn't been typical. She'd been responsible, smart, and determined to make a better life by following Sylvia's example. "Venezuela isn't exactly known for reliable infrastructure." Ana's mind was spinning. "If her parents were here, so close…" She looked to Dana.

The school principal brushed at the red fringe of her bangs. "Josie would've lost her position at our school if we'd found out her parents lived nearby. I can't blame her and the Windermeres for hiding that fact and I commend her for finding a job to help out her parents."

"Sylvia thought the world of Josie." At Laney's sharp glance Ana wished she could reel the words back in. "They cleaned the clinic together a couple of times." Ana traced the curve of her wine glass, wondering how best to proceed. Jumping the gun could cost her, yes, but it could also be a detriment to the investigation if she sent Laney down the wrong path.

This town needed answers about the crisis, not more drama from the doctor they counted on to be calm and collected. When no one else seemed eager to continue the discussion about Josie or Sylvia, Ana steered the conversation in a less volatile direction, grateful when Dana picked up the cues with talk of the upcoming

Fall Carnival for the school. Dana even managed to wrangle a few volunteer hours out of each of them for the event.

"I'm going by Batter Up tomorrow," Dana said. "Hopefully Heidi is willing to donate a cake for the cake walk booth and," she crossed her fingers, "cupcakes for the bake sale table."

"Better you than me," Julia said. "The woman can hardly be civil to me."

"I need to speak with her as well," Laney said. "Let me know when you're done."

"What did she do, shoplift butter?" Julia joked.

Ana hoped not. At her last physical, Heidi's bad cholesterol levels were on the high end.

Laney gave them her *I'm-not-at-liberty-to-say* look. "Nothing like that. Considering how prickly she's been lately, I don't want her turning down Dana because I put her in a bad mood."

"She's either prickly or chattering like a hen." Julia flicked her fingers. "There's a reason I prefer The Grind. Nolan and his staff are steady."

"The investigation has everyone on edge," Ana said. Her hours meant she didn't get to the bakery often, thank goodness. One taste of Heidi's chocolate delight frosting and she'd been hooked. Well aware of her weakness for decadent sweets, Ana typically saved Batter Up treats for the quarterly birthday parties at the clinic.

The rain had finally moved out of the area by the time the four of them settled the check and headed to the parking lot to go their separate ways. Ana stopped Laney before she could move toward her vehicle. "I didn't want to ask in front of the others. When do you think the Coles can claim Sylvia's body?"

She couldn't breach confidentiality and tell Laney outright that it would help Yolanda, but it was a no-brainer that a mother would want to lay her only child to rest.

"I'm sure it will be soon. The report was filed and evidence collected. I'll call the coroner first thing in the morning and lean a little."

"Thank you, Laney."

At her car, Ana slid behind the wheel and just sat there for a minute. Staring out into the darkness, the streets gleaming after the rain, she knew what she had to do. Once her contingency plan was in order, she would write out everything for Laney. What she knew, what she suspected, and how it might tie everything together.

Then she'd leave before Laney was forced to lock her up. It wasn't ideal, deceiving her friends, but it was her only hope to stay ahead of the nightmares she'd been running from for the past twenty-six years.

CHAPTER TWO

The drive home was too brief to gain any insight into the troubling issues. Ana parked in the drive and cut the engine, her thoughts still spinning. Through the years, she'd found a long, quiet drive immensely helpful, allowing her problems to percolate in the back of her mind while she focused on the roadway. This rugged, gorgeous area allowed her plenty of scenic options—she just had to make the time. Despite the days growing shorter, maybe she could get away tomorrow after the press conference in time to enjoy a sunset drive through the mountains.

A rap on her window had her jumping, heart slamming against her ribcage. Griff McCabe, the Shutter Lake Chief of Police, motioned for her to roll down the window.

"You okay?" he asked when she complied.

"No." Ana breathed in the brisk air, letting the soft damp of the autumn night cool her heated cheeks. "I mean, yes. Of course. Just lost in thought." She breathed in again, realizing McCabe didn't smell of beer or fresh mouthwash. It was difficult to assess in the darkness, but his eyes might even be clear, rather than bloodshot per the usual. "What are you doing here?"

It was common knowledge in Shutter Lake that the chief spent most of his evenings pouring beer after beer into his body at The Rabbit Hole. From what she heard, the pattern was occasionally interrupted by a shot of whiskey. He didn't come to her wellness classes and as far as she could tell, his only effort at exercise came from the walk home from the bar each night. None of her advanced medical degrees were necessary to diagnose that the man was troubled.

Year after year at his mandatory annual physicals she'd urged him to back off the copious amounts of alcohol. There were treatment options he could benefit from without risking the position that suited him so well.

"Chief?"

"Your alarm system went off. The company called the station to respond. I was closer than the officer on duty."

Too many things struck her as wrong about his reply. First, The Rabbit Hole was a windowless pub just off the town square and a block away from the police station. Technically, anyone in the station would have been closer to her house. Unless McCabe had been on this side of town already. She and Laney had been physically closer as well, though Laney was off duty.

"I wasn't informed of the alarm," she said, voicing the safest response. She checked her phone, confirming the lack of messages.

His brow puckered over eyes that were often warm when not glazed from alcohol. "I can't speak to that, but I have walked the perimeter. Looks clear now." Griff was an attractive man and good at his job when he was on the clock. It was the hours of downtime he couldn't seem to cope with. She wished Laney was here instead.

"Let me call them."

"Sure." He opened her car door and stepped back to give her room. "One of the motion-detector flood lights out back was the issue according to dispatch. No other sign of trouble out here."

She listened to his report, waiting for the alarm company to answer as they walked to her front door. As he'd said, there were no obvious signs of a break-in. Her hand trembled as she simultaneously unlocked her door and gave the customer service rep who'd answered her address and information.

The young man on the other end of the line was kind and professional as he confirmed McCabe's story and apologized that the text alerts she'd set up for her account had not gone through. She thanked him and ended the call. It was ridiculous to feel as if the police had cornered her, but she couldn't help it after the speculation in Laney's gaze earlier and the chief's surprise appearance.

Standing out on her front porch with McCabe at her back, a chill washed over her. By mid-October the nights were downright nippy. At the clinic, she would have invited him into her office, but this was her home. Unfortunately, he didn't seem in a hurry to get back to his normal beer-guzzling routine. "Where's your car?"

He shifted a bit, as if he expected to see his vehicle in her driveway. "Oh. I parked down the road." With his mouth edging toward a smile, he tipped his head in the direction of Sylvia's home. "So I wouldn't scare anyone off."

"I see." Her hand wrapped around the doorknob. "Thank you for responding." She regretted the stiffness in her voice. "It was probably a raccoon. They set off the lights once in a while."

He tucked his hands into his jacket pockets. "Dr. Perez, I'm happy to take a look around inside before I go if that will ease your mind."

Hardly. "You said there weren't any signs of trouble."

"I've only walked around outside."

She wasn't sure if he was trying to scare her or if he hoped to find something incriminating lying about in plain sight. That was paranoia tickling the back of her throat, making her palms damp. She'd done nothing wrong. Or rather, she'd done nothing that resulted in direct harm to Sylvia or anyone else.

"I'll be fine." She forced her lips into a smile. "Do you need a lift back to your car?"

"No, thanks. I can walk."

"All right." She waited. He stayed rooted to the spot. "Is there something else?"

He sighed and scrubbed a hand over his face. "Medical records," he said. "I couldn't get the body from the river out of my mind. Did you ever treat Josie Rodriguez?"

It wasn't the question she expected. "No. But a full medical history with a vaccination record would've been part of the exchange student requirements. I'm sure the school has that on file."

"Right. Dr. Perkins sent that over. Unless they took a DNA sample too, it won't help us with identification. So far we're drawing a blank on finding her dental records."

"I'm sorry." Ana inched toward the door again. McCabe wasn't taking the hint. "If you'll excuse me?"

"Actually, I wanted to ask about my medical records too."

She felt her jaw drop and snapped her mouth closed. Resigned, she opened the front door. "We should go inside."

"You keep records here?" He closed the door behind him.

She did her best to recall he was an officer of the law, no need to brace for an attack. "No." Flipping the light switch, she set her purse on the hall tree, keeping her cell phone in hand. "I prefer to keep business and home separate."

"Don't we all," he muttered.

"It really is the healthier choice."

He murmured his agreement, his gaze roaming over the space. "Wow. I'd heard... but this is some perk."

"The council insisted I should be comfortable." The house, with all its custom, luxurious finishes set on a serene, wooded lot had been a significant part of her decision to lead the Shutter Lake Medical Clinic.

Dark, rustic beams emphasized the vaulted ceilings. A fireplace framed by river rock divided the living and dining areas. The long table, a custom piece made from reclaimed wood, could comfortably seat ten. The earthy, neutral tones of her décor made a gentle backdrop for the vibrant artwork she'd gathered through the years. In the daylight, the trees that ensured her privacy offered a living, ever-changing canvas through the wall of windows and doors that opened to a sprawling deck. The kitchen, furnished with only the best appliances and finishes, was a masterpiece as well, turning what she'd often viewed as a chore into a delight.

He checked windows and doors, finding everything locked up tight, taking it all in.

Looking at her home as a newcomer might, she felt a familiar swell of pride with equally familiar doubt creeping along the edges. No one could argue she'd done well, overcoming tremendous odds as an Hispanic woman in America's competitive medical field. Regardless of the years separating her from the crowded barrio of her youth, she worried about the long slide back down if anyone discovered her secret.

Nothing she'd learned or accomplished could balance what she'd done. Because it clouded her perspective, she didn't dwell on it often.

Although Sylvia had often teased her that the house was far too much for one person day to day, Ana never regretted having all this room. It was an ideal home for entertaining. In addition to the annual cook out for the city council to discuss new treatment options and tools and present her equipment requests, she hosted game nights for clinic employees as well as the holiday gathering that had become a much-loved tradition.

"Would you like coffee?" she asked before he moved down the hallway to the bedrooms.

"Hmm?" Clearly distracted, he turned slowly away from the framed print of a Yolanda deCosta painting. "Oh. No, thanks."

To her eye, the red-roofed village tucked into the green mountains in the painting was the best blend of where she'd come from and where she'd landed. "You had some question about your medical records?" she prompted.

His hands caressed the marble countertop. Those broad hands, callused and scarred, told a story of a man who enjoyed digging into projects outside of his work as the chief of police. She wondered why he'd stopped working on cars and now filled his free time with drinking.

"Yes." He drew his hands back, as if he'd realized what he revealed. "I'd like to know what's in my record."

His annual physical wasn't due for several months. "Have you been feeling ill?"

"Am I an alcoholic?"

"Yes," she answered immediately. He sank onto one of the stools that ran the length of the island. No longer afraid he was going to prod her about Sylvia or anything more personal, she rounded the counter to join him. "That can't be a shock, Griff. I've brought it up before."

"Have you documented it so bluntly in my file?"

"No." Was he looking for another job? If it was the job that drove him to drink, she wasn't sure his body could handle a place with more stress. Shutter Lake was the least stressful place she'd known, until murder cracked the façade. "Are you ready to seek treatment?"

"No."

Emphatic as ever. "Then what?"

"In your professional opinion, does my drinking impact my work?" He braced an elbow on the countertop, as if her answer didn't matter at all, but she saw the tension in the lines bracketing his mouth, the set of his jaw. "Well?"

This was a conversation she'd be happier having at the clinic, with her lab coat on, surrounded by people who could assist if he turned surly. "I rarely see you at work," she began. "You seem to have the respect of Deputy Chief Holt and the other officers in the department. Together, it seems you handle the responsibilities quite well."

He slapped the counter. "Stop spoon-feeding me what you think I want to hear."

"I've never done that." She hoped her exaggerated calm defused his sudden temper. "Maybe you should ask me whatever it is you really want to know."

"I want to know if someone is killing women here or dumping bodies in our back yard because they've heard I'm inept." Agitated, he shoved to his feet. "Everyone knows I'm out of my depth on the Cole case. Now that girl…" His voice trailed off.

"Griff." He paced to the windows that overlooked the deck and flipped on the flood light, tested the locked handle. "Chief McCabe."

He continued to ignore her, checking the window over the kitchen sink. She wished Dana were here. She always seemed to have the right words when people of any age were facing a crisis. Her expertise revolved around the body and its systems. Sure the brain was a piece of that puzzle, but she preferred dealing with test results and facts rather than raw emotions.

He stalked off down the hallway before she could stop him. She trailed in his wake as he checked the windows in each bedroom, her office, and the baths as well. It wasn't much of a privacy invasion. Still, she struggled against that old sensation of being violated, judged, and found lacking.

Her issues had no bearing or relevance here. Clinic setting or not, this visit was more about *his* issues than the possibility of a break in. "Are you looking for something in particular?" Unless he picked apart her computer or discovered the false bottom in her lower desk drawer, her secrets were safe. For tonight.

"No." He glowered at her, his hands on his hips.

"Are you trying to prove something?"

His expression eased. "I might drink more than I should, but I know my job."

The same line he offered at every physical. "Good." They might as well be on a stage, they had the routine down so well.

"I've never handled a murder investigation," he said quietly. "Laney has the lead on this case for a reason. Now there are two dead bodies and one person still missing. Shutter Lake needs better than me."

Tell him.

She ignored that pesky inner voice. This was not the time to be naïve or give in to fear. In his current mood, she thought he'd answer any question she posed, though he shouldn't discuss the case with anyone outside the department. Beyond the legalities and protocols, she didn't really want to shoulder the burden of his doubts about the case or his concerns about her neighbors and patients as suspects.

"None of that is on you," Ana said with all the confidence she could muster. "No one could have seen this coming."

With the possible exception of Sylvia. In recent weeks, after Josie had suddenly returned to Venezuela, her friend had been increasingly worried. Convinced the girl was in some kind of trouble, she'd spoken with Ana on more than one occasion about how best to bring her back to the states.

"I wonder," Griff muttered.

"Come back to the kitchen," she suggested. "I'll make you a hot chocolate." Her machine had all the bells and whistles and sometimes it was fun to indulge in something more than a basic cup of black coffee.

"I suppose it's better than coffee at this hour."

Or beer. She kept the thought to herself. "Fall is hot chocolate weather."

"Especially tonight," he agreed.

Her shoulders relaxed a bit more with every step they took away from her office. Settled at the counter again, she could feel him watching her as she prepped the comforting treat.

"Marshmallows?" she asked as the machine sputtered the last of the foam into his cup.

He cocked an eyebrow at her. "*You* have marshmallows?"

"I'm not a complete ogre about sugar," she replied.

He snorted. "I smell a trap."

She tilted her head and noticed his gaze following the sway of her ponytail. A distinct awareness rippled between them. It happened occasionally though neither of them ever drifted down that path of mutual attraction. "Is that a yes or a no?"

"Yes."

Those earnest eyes that smiled too rarely were daring her to prove she kept sweets in the house. She felt him watching as she strolled to her pantry, stepped in and pulled out a squat canister of mini-marshmallows. Without a word, she set the canister between them on the counter and opened it.

"Wow." He reached in and grabbed several, setting them afloat in the aromatic chocolate. "This is *big* news," he teased. "How much will you pay me to not tell Julia Ford?"

Smothering a laugh, Ana stirred several marshmallows into her own mug of chocolate. "She already knows."

Feigning dismay, Griff groaned. "Of course she does. Girl-friends always know the secrets."

Ana wasn't sure how to respond. It should have been casual banter, easily discarded. Was he about to shift this to an interrogation? "Surely men share their inner thoughts and desires as well," she said.

The look he gave her—utterly horrified—made it impossible to retain any of her typical composure. She laughed until she snorted, only to laugh some more.

"I've never seen you laugh that way," he observed when she finally recovered.

She sat up straight, pinned him with her most direct, medical-expert gaze. "In the clinic and at the wellness events I am expected to be a professional."

"Of course." He glared into his mug for a long moment before lifting his eyes to meet hers. "You keep business and personal space separate."

"I try."

"Maybe you shouldn't." He studied her over the rim of his mug. Sipped slowly. "Laughter looks good on you, doctor."

She laughed at the clinic. Granted, not to the point of snorting, but she laughed. "Thanks," she managed, flustered by his scrutiny. "It feels like a long time since I've had a big laugh."

"You're not alone," he said. He looked up and when his gaze met hers she caught the full force of the heat in his eyes. "I am sorry you lost your good friend."

Her throat too dry to speak, she bobbed her chin.

He reached out and covered her hand with his. Warmth and strength spread through her system from that point of contact. It was a touch that held a question as well as the first glimpse of a real promise. She didn't move, didn't take her eyes off his, though desire throbbed with an achy need pulsing just under her skin.

In this situation, what she wanted and what she could have were not compatible. If —when—her secrets came out, any personal association with her would wreck his career faster than his Rabbit

Hole habit. Self-sabotage was one thing. She would not run the risk of contributing to his downfall.

"All right." He pulled back, tucked his hands into his pockets. "Thanks for the hot chocolate." He carried his mug to the sink. "I'll cut back on the alcohol."

The statement stunned her and he was nearly to her front door before she trusted her quivering knees to hold her upright. "Griff." He paused, one hand on the doorknob. "If you need help with that, come see me."

"Sure thing, doc." He tilted his head toward the door. "Lock up behind me and reset your alarm."

Her heart still racing, she did as he asked, listening to his footsteps fade into the chilly night.

CHAPTER THREE

Monday October 15

Laney stepped out of the police station, grateful for the clear air and sunshine. She was happy for the walk after missing her run last night due to the rain and wine with the girls. Predictably she'd woken antsy and on edge. A dead body had that effect on her. As news spread today that they'd pulled a young woman from the river, that dead body was likely to have an effect on everyone in town.

She shifted her focus as she walked along. The songbirds were lively today, filling the morning with happy calls and bright chatter that was completely at odds with her pensive mood.

The world always smelled better to her after a good, hard rain as if the weather was determined to wash away some of the dark stains people left behind. According to the preliminary report from the Nevada County coroner, the river had certainly done it's best to wash any evidence from the body they'd found yesterday.

That posed a problem. They were stumped already on the Sylvia Cole case. All they had was what they'd deduced from the crime scene and the coroner's report. Sylvia's front door had been unlocked and left ajar, suggesting she'd invited her attacker into her home. The lack of defensive wounds along with the angle, force and damage to the victim's throat as a result of the strangulation, led them to believe they were looking for a tall, strong man. Despite the signs of a struggle, the odds were high she'd known her killer. Sure her wallet had been emptied, but no one was using the plastic so that seemed like a red herring to Laney.

They had even less to go on with the newly recovered body that was most likely Josie Rodriguez. Laney had seen cases solved with less to go on, but not many. The last thing this town needed was two unsolved murders blotting the previously perfect record of non-violence.

She crossed the town square admiring the colorful mums, sheaves of wheat, and pumpkins that had been repurposed after the annual benefit concert for the arts. The temporary stage was gone, along with the chairs, the catering tent and the vendor displays, but the general uplifting energy remained. Community was one thing Shutter Lake did exceptionally well, consistently.

Even with an unsolved murder, people were sticking together. Not to cover for a criminal as some seedier neighborhoods did in L.A., but in support of those most affected. She'd seen the outpouring of concern for Sylvia's parents at the press conferences as well as at events like Saturday's benefit and it restored a bit of her faith in people.

When she reached the door to Batter Up, she smoothed back strands of her hair that the autumn breeze teased loose. She walked in and joined the line. Heidi Udall, owner of the bakery, was behind the counter chattering away as she served a customer perusing the day's offering.

Heidi baked what she wanted each day, in whatever amounts suited her. In the two years Laney had lived here, she'd never seen the baker make an effort to follow a schedule or track her bestselling items. The lack of strategy didn't seem to be hurting business, considering the cluster of customers.

"Hi, Laney!" Heidi called brightly. "I'll be right with you."

"No rush," Laney said. She'd use the delay as an opportunity to observe Heidi's customers, noting who picked up an individual treat and who was picking up for groups.

She waited near the Halloween scene decorating the front window, careful not to block anyone's view from the street. Heidi had a reputation for being testy about things that she perceived interrupted her business. A bit lumpy and limp, her hat askew, the witch looked as if she'd put up a good resistance to being on display.

As she adjusted the witch's hat, Laney watched Heidi zip around behind the counter with almost too much cheer. Had the woman dumped too much sugar or an extra shot of espresso into the tall cup of coffee by the register? Maybe both?

Clearly some of the bakery's customers were regulars and naturally, the size of the town meant they all knew each other well enough to say hello. Laney held the door for Lou Branson. Clearly a Monday person, he happily told her that part of his role as the bank manager was picking up the cake for the monthly birthday party.

The wait dragged on and she started to feel more like Batter Up's doorman than a deputy chief as customers came and went. The bakery shared an alley with The Grind coffee shop and Laney was half-tempted to dash over and grab another cup of coffee. If she did that, she'd only get grief from Heidi. The woman was ridiculously competitive with the coffee shop owner, Nolan Ikard, and that would put her in a foul mood when Laney needed her to cooperate.

Her patience waning, Laney waited for two more people who walked in to be served before she had Heidi alone. "Looks like you might need to hire counter help."

Heidi fanned her face. Sweat glistened along her forehead, dampened the gray hair curling at her temples from under the edge of the baker's hat. "The morning rush starts my day off right." She raised the tall reusable mug of coffee. "Better than this, actually."

Laney smiled as her long-underused instincts fired to life. The baker was nervous, high, or both. In her experience that was a bad combination for a suspect and a potential goldmine for an investigator.

Heidi snapped a napkin from the dispenser and blotted her face as the bells over the door jingled. "Welcome to Batter Up!" She crumpled the damp napkin and shoved it into her apron pocket as she rattled off the day's special.

Laney greeted Renata Fernandez. She'd been Sylvia's second in command and now kept things running at Sparkle until the business aspects could be sorted out for clients and employees. They spoke for a few minutes about weather and Halloween plans, carefully avoiding any mention of unpleasant topics. Once again Laney hoped the body from the river would give them a lead, but she couldn't plant false hope.

"Will there be a press conference tonight?" Renata asked.

"That's the plan." With luck they could announce real progress rather than another vague update on the investigation.

When Renata walked out, Laney flipped the sign to CLOSED.

"You can't do that!" Heidi exclaimed, marching around the counter.

Laney recognized the signs of drug-induced bravado, under-scored by the dilated pupils and nervous intensity. "What are you on, Heidi?"

The baker sputtered. "I'm not *on* anything, but I *am* in business, Deputy Chief Holt. Flip that sign."

"In just a minute," Laney said, her tone cool and even. "When we found Sylvia Cole's body, the crime scene unit inventoried her home. Par for the course," she explained. "At that time, a dozen Batter Up cupcakes were boxed in her refrigerator. I came in to ask if she ordered them for an event or something."

"Sylvia often bought cupcakes for her employees," Heidi said.

"Generous of her. I'm sure the girls appreciated that."

"They did." The baker's chin came up. "If you ask me everyone at Sparkle could stand to eat a cupcake more often. You too."

Laney ignored the envious barb. Sylvia had been cover-model gorgeous and she hired women who matched her in both beauty and work ethic. "Can you show me the receipt for Sylvia's order, please? She must have picked up the order on the third to take to the office on the fourth."

"No." Heidi folded her arms over her ample bosom.

"No," Laney echoed.

Heidi's lips curled into a manic smile. "I mean, I'd love to show you the receipt, of course." She unfolded her arms and drummed her hands restlessly against her thighs, dusting her pants with floured fingerprints. "But my computer system was giving me fits at the end of September. Fiscal year and all that blah, blah, blah."

"You don't have any sales records for this October?" Laney didn't believe that for a second.

"Oh, sure I do. Just not here and definitely not off the top of my head." She tapped her temple, drawing Laney's eye to a slightly swollen, discolored spot on her forehead. "Ask me anything about a recipe and it's a steel trap up here, b—"

"When did you bump your head?"

"What? Oh, this?" She flapped a hand in front of her face. "Tripped when I got up in the night."

"Ran into a door?" Laney queried.

"Yes," Heidi replied, the sarcasm sailing right over her head. "How'd you know?"

"I've seen similar injuries before." The baker's personal life wasn't really her business, but she hadn't heard anything about a recent relationship. In fact the woman was notoriously single. "Did you have Dr. Perez or someone at the clinic check it out?" she asked as Heidi took another slug of her coffee.

"No. It's a bump. I'm more embarrassed than injured."

"Head injuries can be tricky." Though in Laney's experience they didn't usually cause this sort of mania. "When did it happen?" she asked, adding a thick layer of 'concerned community servant' to the query. She was far more interested in getting behind the counter for a good look around. If Heidi was sober, Laney would turn in her badge and resign today.

"Thursday or Friday, I think."

"If you can't pin it down, I'll walk with you to the clinic."

"I don't need a doctor," Heidi exclaimed. "It must have been Friday. At least the bruise was enough at that point that I applied cover up before the benefit on Saturday. There, see. I'm fine."

"You sure are. Thanks." The timing matched up with the night the cupcakes walked out of the crime scene. Assuming Heidi was the culprit, why would she steal back her own cupcakes?

"Is that all? I really shouldn't ignore my customers much longer."

Laney glanced toward the front door. No one was waiting on the sidewalk. All of the locals were familiar with Heidi's whims about business hours.

"I'll need that sales report as soon as possible." Laney pursed her lips. "Do you ever give refunds?"

Heidi gasped, the reaction dramatic enough for a Hollywood screen test. "No one has ever had reason to ask for a refund. I do excellent work."

"I agree," Laney held up her hands in surrender. "Your cupcakes are addictive." She waited while the baker preened. "Well, I just can't figure out how or why the cupcakes in Sylvia's refrigerator disappeared."

"I'm sure one of your crime scene people ate them. There was a selection of my most popular flavors in that box."

"You're sure?"

"Of course I'm sure. I made Strawberry, Chocolate Delight, Butter Cream and Caramel too."

She could remember what she baked, but not how the sale was made? Laney's instincts went into high gear. "So you remember Sylvia placing the order. Did she pick it up or did you deliver?" Laney doubted that Heidi made a habit of deliveries.

"What?" Clearly agitated, Heidi bit her lip and then sipped her coffee. "I don't deliver. Not exactly. Only to Mr. Duval. Due to a special, standing order."

"Hmm. If I'm following correctly, Sylvia picked up the cupcakes the day before she was killed and took them home rather than to the office right here in town." She jerked her thumb toward the east, in the general direction of the Sparkle office located in a building on the street past the police station.

Heidi frowned. "Yes. That sounds right. She normally picked up an assortment of whatever was available for her girls."

"Oh." Laney mirrored Heidi's confusion. "So she didn't place a special order on the third for your most popular flavors."

"Umm, no." Heidi replied through gritted teeth. "I'll look for the receipt this afternoon. Sylvia would usually ask for an extra Chocolate Delight after she hired Josie."

"You don't sound happy about it."

Heidi puffed up her chest and planted her hands on her hips. "It didn't matter a bit to me. The girl would come in here nearly every day for her chocolate fix regardless."

"I can relate," Laney said. "Like I said, your cupcakes are addictive."

Instead of preening under the praise, this time Heidi's eyes took on a calculating gleam. She reached for a box. "Will you be taking one or two dozen cupcakes back to the station?"

"I walked over, so only one dozen. An assortment will do, but make sure we have at least two of the pumpkin cheesecake flavor." She tapped the glass case. "It's Officer Trask's favorite."

"It's a seasonal bestseller."

"I appreciate your time, Heidi." Laney waited a beat while the baker nestled each cupcake into the box with care. "Who's your supplier?"

Heidi bobbled the box, recovering quickly. "That depends. Paper goods come from one service, foodstuffs from another. Whenever I can, I use locally grown produce."

"And what about the cocaine? Where do you get that?"

Heidi slammed the box onto the counter, negating all her earlier care with her product. "You need to leave right now. I have the right to refuse service."

"I'll go." Laney held up her hands. "Just as soon as you call Dr. Perez to set up a rehab program."

"I do *not* need rehab!" Heidi shrieked.

"Says every addict ever." Laney felt a pang of sympathy. "Being in business poses all kinds of challenges," she said gently. "You're not the first to resort to a chemical booster."

"Get out of my store!" She flung her arm toward the door.

Laney pointed at the phone on the wall behind her. "Call Dr. Perez, get into treatment and I'll lock up for you."

"I will not be treated this way, Deputy Chief Holt," she blustered. "You've crossed a line." She tore off her apron, flung it over the register. "Chief McCabe will deal with you."

Laney was ready when Heidi turned and bolted for the back door. She had agility and speed on her side. Being high might have increased Heidi's alertness, but it impaired her judgment. Rather than simply run, she stopped for her purse and got the strap tangled with the hook. As she wrestled to get free, her purse upended. Keys, sunglasses, lip gloss, wallet, loose change and several unmistakable packets of white powder spilled out across the floor.

As she tried to scoop up everything, Laney caught her hands and cuffed her, shoving her into the corner.

"Don't do this," she pleaded, tears rolling down her round cheeks. "You'll ruin me."

"No, that's on you. You're an adult. You know there are consequences for every decision."

"I'm not a bad person," Heidi spluttered. "I haven't hurt anyone."

"Drugs hurt a community one junkie at a time." She dropped to one knee in front of Heidi. "Who is your supplier?" Based on the amount of coke in her purse, this was more than occasional recreational use. She had enough on her to support an active daily habit.

Yes, the SLPD had a murder, probably two, to solve, but Laney refused to give an inch on crime right now. Murder and drugs often went hand in hand. Shutter Lake didn't need another scandal compounding the current crisis.

When Heidi didn't answer her, she dialed the medical clinic and asked to speak with Ana.

"I'm in the middle of a drug intervention," Laney said when Ana answered. "Can you send an ambulance over to Batter Up, please? Heidi needs a treatment program."

"I do not!" she shouted. "I won't go!"

"If she refuses treatment..."

Laney sighed as Ana's voice trailed off. No need to finish that thought. Glaring down at Heidi, she made a decision. "She has a head injury as well. Possible concussion."

Heidi swore. "Liar!"

"I'll send a team to pick her up, "Ana replied. "I can't guarantee she'll stay."

Laney thought about the baker's aggressive reactions and brash attitude. "Let's give her a chance to calm down. Have them come to the back door. I'll explain her options on the criminal side of things, if she refuses my generous offer."

She pressed a finger to her ear as Heidi burst into another flood of tears. "Thanks for the assist," she said to Ana, ending the call.

Crouching again, she stared at Heidi. Her face red and splotchy, her eyes still showed the signs of drug use. "You still have choices. I can take you to the station and start the legal proceedings—"

"For what? I'm a user, not a dealer. No one got hurt!"

"The amount you're carrying around, this could go either way. Or," Laney continued, "we can skip the public humiliation of that and you can take a medical approach."

"You'll charge me either way," Heidi spat. "I'll file a complaint. You're interfering with my business. Planting drugs on my person. You're working for Nolan!"

Paranoia was another classic symptom of drug abuse. "All right, we'll go to the station." She hauled Heidi to her feet. "Heidi Udall, you're under arrest for possession of cocaine with possible intent to distribute. You have the right to remain silent…"

"Wait! Wait!" Heidi gulped in a breath.

"Laney, please." She wiped her face on her shoulder. "I didn't do anything wrong. If you take me to the clinic, I'll go into a program."

"And?"

"And what?"

Laney wanted nothing more than to roll her eyes. She had to take what she could get right now. "Is your supplier in Shutter Lake?"

"No."

"Thank you." One small victory she and McCabe would celebrate. "I will search your bakery and I am going to pursue those missing cupcakes."

"Whatever."

"Is there anyone I can call to handle the perishables?"

"Now you're nice?" Heidi puffed a breath that lifted her bangs. "I'll talk with my *doctor* about the details."

"Works for me."

When the ambulance arrived, Laney saw Heidi loaded in, gave the key for the cuffs to the attendants and watched them drive away.

Shaking her head, she turned back to the daunting task of searching Heidi's bakery kitchen for drugs and the link between Sylvia's cupcake order and the disappearance of those cupcakes.

While searching for Sylvia's killer, they'd found she wasn't simply the beautiful entrepreneur loved by her staff. Sylvia had been black-mailing several of her clients. According to interviews with the employees, Heidi remained a Sparkle client. Lucy Gomez had taken over her service. Had Sylvia learned about the cocaine habit and used it to squeeze the baker in order to add to the stacks of cash they'd found in the wall safe?

It fit. Shaking her head, Laney called McCabe. This search would go better with two of them. She had no intention of giving Heidi any loopholes to slip through on the drug charge or anything else.

CHAPTER FOUR

Ana had learned early on that Mondays posed challenges for medical professionals. Even in Shutter Lake, where the overwhelming majority of citizens were committed to a healthy lifestyle, patients often waited for office hours rather than seek care over a weekend. Even though she rarely went out of town and could be on site within minutes, people too often waited for regular hours. Add in the patients who overdid it with sports or various physically demanding projects and the waiting room was always full on Mondays.

She and her team had barely cleared the most urgent cases when Laney called for help with Heidi Udall. While the team picked up the patient, Ana juggled the scheduled appointments so she could handle the baker's crisis personally.

The signs of habitual drug use were clear enough and Ana chided herself for not noticing sooner. The health of this community rested on her shoulders. To be fair, she didn't cross paths with Heidi often since the woman avoided the wellness activities and regular checkups. Now Ana had a better understanding of why.

Belligerent and embarrassed despite every effort to protect her privacy, Heidi reluctantly agreed to enter a drug rehabilitation program. She only had two conditions, the first being she didn't have to talk with Deputy Chief Holt again. Ana didn't make any guarantees, only assuring her that no one from the SLPD would violate her rights.

The second condition was that Ana find someone to take a cupcake or doughnut to Troy Duval and visit with him each week. She explained how she inherited the thoughtful task from Sylvia and Dana picked up the tab for the treats now.

Accepting Ana's promise to fulfill those conditions, Heidi asked to call Sheena Appleton, her backup baker. Ana allowed the phone call and then finished the arrangements for Heidi's transfer. She and the staff were just getting back on schedule when Nolan walked in.

Since Sylvia's death, the owner of The Grind coffee shop had been suffering physically. Although his symptoms mirrored a stomach virus, Ana suspected the root of his trouble was grief. As both physician and friend, she knew Nolan had been sleeping with Sylvia. Her friend claimed it was more convenience than relationship. Ana wasn't sure Nolan would have agreed with that definition.

When she met him in the exam room, she could tell by his gray pallor and the deep circles under his eyes that nothing had improved. "No change?" she asked.

"Dr. Perez, there has to be a pill or something that will work." He pulled his dark hoodie tight around his torso, huddling as if he couldn't get warm enough.

Time, she thought. Only time could heal the erosion of grief. "You're not running a fever—"

"I can't keep anything down."

"I understand," she soothed. "I miss her too."

He gawked at her. "You... what? What are you talking about?"

"In my professional opinion your symptoms are just as likely to be emotional as viral. Every test we've run has come back clear, Nolan."

"She told you about me?" His voice cracked and he cleared his throat. "Sylvia told you about me?"

Ana nodded.

"What did she say?"

"Good things." Ana smiled, grateful her dusky-gold complexion rarely revealed her emotions. "Good things," she repeated absently.

Sylvia had never made a habit of sharing all the intimate, gritty details of her sex life, not even with Ana. But she'd made it clear she enjoyed her time with Nolan immensely.

He slouched in the chair, his long legs stretched out and his hands over his face. "I loved her, Dr. Perez. I loved her and I don't know what to do now."

Tears leaked around his fingers, dampening his cheeks and the beard he hadn't shaved for several days. "You're doing exactly what you need to do," she assured him. "Cry. Shout. Take some time off. Talk to a friend. Grief needs an outlet."

"There's no one to talk to. No one who has any idea how close we were. How she…"

His voice trailed off, his gaze distant, proving that was the crux of it. Nolan was carrying a terrible burden all by himself. According to Sylvia one of Nolan's biggest assets had been his discretion. He respected and honored her request to keep their hook-ups private. Neither of them could have foreseen this scenario and how complete discretion hurt him.

Ana thought of Sylvia's visits with Troy Duval, a secret she hadn't known about. It was a quirk of Sylvia's to keep so many things private and compartmentalized, from business to people. At first glance that seemed like an excellent philosophy. One she too had adopted early in her life. Now Ana wasn't so sure. "You can talk to me," she said before she could change her mind.

Nolan's gaze cleared, sharpened. He sat forward in a flurry of long limbs. "Whatever I say here is confidential, right?"

"Yes." Ana managed not to recoil at the abrupt and intense change in his demeanor. Was Nolan suffering so deeply because he'd killed Sylvia? *Please not that.* "Yes," she repeated. "Unless you share information about a crime or show me signs that you're a threat to yourself or others."

The surge of energy and enthusiasm drained away as swiftly as it had appeared. He slumped back into the chair again. "You think I killed her."

Her hands still folded on the desktop in front of her, Ana studied the man, first as a patient and then as a friend of a friend. She made the effort to remain objective, keeping her old fears buried.

"No." She'd seen killers up close. She'd looked into the eyes of killers who believed they loved their victims. The memories pulsed to the surface like a slow-moving bubble of lava ready to burst and spill over, scorching her. She pushed back, focusing on the present. "If you know something about who *did* kill her, I encourage you to speak up."

"To you?" Hope flared in his grief-worn gaze.

"To the authorities, preferably. Sylvia deserves justice."

Nolan leaned forward, elbows braced on his knees. "Yes, she does."

"As someone who loved her," Ana continued, "you understand the need for closure."

"I know. Believe me, if I could help the investigation, I would."

"All right." Ana didn't press further. She wished there was more she could do, for Nolan and Sylvia. "Did you try the herbal tea I suggested?"

He sat up, sheepish. "It helped a little," he admitted. "Lacks flavor."

"Add some honey." He could stand the boost and calories from a little sugar right now. "And pick up some chocolate."

"I don't really have a sweet tooth," he said.

"Then bring the chocolate for me when you come in for a follow up." The joke brought out a ghost of his charming smile. The response gave her confidence he'd soon be through this acute phase of the grieving process. If only she could say the same for Sylvia's parents. Or even herself.

At the door, Nolan paused. "How do you do it, doc?"

"Do what?"

He circled a finger around his own face. "Keep up the cool, confident façade."

"A lifetime of practice." She smiled, sincerely, just to prove she still could. "Medical school is really just several long, intense years of poker-face training."

She and Sylvia had both mastered that exhausting aspect of being successful in a service industry. It required effort and commitment to remain calm and professional when clients were in a tizzy or a crisis. No wonder they'd bonded so quickly.

"So nothing rattles you?" Nolan asked.

"Oh, I wouldn't say that." She patted Nolan's shoulder. Premature death bugged her almost as much as physical affection. Unsolved murders definitely rattled her. "We all grow up, but everyone still has a monster or two lurking under the bed."

"Guess so." Shoulders hunched again, Nolan turned and walked out of the exam room.

She stood there in the wake of his sadness wondering what to do next. Sylvia had told her she'd taken precautions during her search for answers to Josie's disappearance. She'd promised to set up some sort of alert or message that would deliver to Ana if something terrible happened.

Well, the absolute *worst* thing had happened and the continued silence was deafening. Could she ask Laney about it or give the deputy chief a lead without digging an inescapable hole for herself?

Not yet.

She couldn't tie any of her suspicions about who killed Sylvia to actual facts. The police didn't need another wild goose chase and supposition wouldn't make a difference for Sylvia, Josie, or even Mr. and Mrs. Cole. As she told everyone who'd asked since the day they found Sylvia's body, she didn't know anything.

"Imbecile! Idiot!" Her father's insults filled her ears and she flinched with the first lash of the belt across her bare back. "Have you learned nothing?"

Silence was the only safe response when he was angry and making a point.

"They are not your pets. They are my property. They are cattle."

Each hard statement was violently underscored with the belt. Pain shot through her as her flesh stung and burned. Wounds on her back meant her sister or mother would have to help her wash. They would all be punished if he found out they did anything to ease her suffering.

She forced her eyes to stay open, to keep still and endure, as he beat her in front of the women chained to the wall. Age was impossible to determine, she only knew they were older than her, with breasts and hair over their privates.

Nothing was private in this room.

The women were only allowed to wash and dress when they were selected to work a job or meet a private client. Her father claimed clothing was a wasted resource that gave them delusions of power and respect.

Her father, Sergio Rojas, held the power. And he made it clear that respect and dignity would never be offered in this dank hole.

Hatred for him burned through her, deeper than the lash and sting of his belt.

At church each week the priest taught them hate was a sin. He told the people filling his church to forgive. She knew she could not. He told them to pray. She did not see the point in prayer anymore. He told the people to know others by their actions and leave vengeance to the Lord.

By his actions, she knew her father was evil. Her nerves on fire with desperation in her heart, she wasn't convinced the Lord would exact vengeance in time to save these women. To save her.

"Dr. Perez? Are you well?"

Ana blinked rapidly, clearing away the gruesome memory. Slowly, the face of Donovan Keller, her newest physician assistant, came into focus. He was young, trim, and well built, with hair more red than blonde. Compassionate and witty, his clear blue eyes sparkled when he smiled, making him an immediate favorite with the female patients.

"*Hmm?*" Based on the tone and concern in his gaze, he'd clearly asked the question more than once. "Yes, I'm fine. Merely lost in thought."

Those clever blue eyes flashed. "It's a Monday."

"Right." She didn't have a better excuse. "Lost thoughts will wait." Checking her watch, she added, "We have a good three hours of clinic left today."

"And about four hours of patients," he quipped. "I'll get moving."

"Me too." Smiling, she moved toward the next exam room.

Ana peeked at her cell phone for any missed messages. Finding none, she stepped into her office and made a quick call before hurrying back into the fray. She didn't want to miss the press conference and a chance to speak with Dana in person.

No matter how she tried to protect both her staff and their patients, once the announcement for a press conference was made, the tension was palpable. A natural effect, even if she didn't like it. Everyone in Shutter Lake hoped to hear the police investigation was progressing.

Everyone but the killer, she thought, as she walked in to meet with her next patient.

At a few minutes past the hour, Ana scooted through the crowd gathered in front of City Hall waiting for the press conference to start. Three weeks now and Ana could see people had established their favorite places, as if this was a new community event rather than a house of horrors disguised by deep blue skies and vibrant autumn color on the trees.

At the podium, Laney stood to the right of Griff who looked decidedly stern and official as Mayor Jessup joined them.

"Have I missed anything?" Ana asked.

"Only the sound check," Dana said.

Ana glanced back toward the podium and thought she had a few more seconds. Leaning closer to Dana again she lowered her voice so they wouldn't be overheard. It wasn't easy to ask about the arrangement with Troy Duval without violating Heidi's privacy, but she tiptoed around the privacy issues to keep her promise to Heidi.

The particulars of fulfilling that promise would have to wait as the Mayor greeted the community gathered in the street. He gave precious few details about either Sylvia's case or the body from the river, instead inviting Chief McCabe to the podium right away.

Ana knew at once what McCabe was about to say. She could see it etched onto his face.

"Through a cooperative effort, the coroner has identified the body pulled from the river as Josie Rodriguez."

A ripple of unease swept over the crowd. Ana swallowed a gasp of fear. The news wasn't a surprise, but that didn't give it any less impact. She pulled out her cell phone and sent a text to her backup teacher for this evening's yoga class. After this news, she needed to juggle her priorities for the sake of herself and her patients.

When Ana returned her attention to the press conference, the mayor was at the podium again, both hands curled tightly around the edges, his lips pressed into a firm line as he collected his thoughts. The expertly-tailored suit couldn't overcome the stark changes that worry had carved on his normal professional friendliness and composure.

"I understand this is a shock to our community," Jessup said. "The loss we're facing is tragic. One of our own, born and raised here and now… Now a bright young woman who aspired to call this area home."

A soft cry carried over the crowd as Yolanda Cole turned into the supportive embrace of her husband Zion.

"Please," the mayor continued, "I implore you, speak up if you have any information about either of these investigations. No detail is too small. Quentin and Katherine Windermere, Josie's family during her time here as an exchange student, have added one million dollars to the current reward for any information on Sylvia Cole's case.

"Our police department is working around the clock to resolve these cases so we can all grieve, heal, and move forward with some measure of confidence and peace."

A low blow, Ana thought, eyeing Laney and Griff. Since when had anyone lost confidence in the SLPD? They were doing all they could, sifting through the facts and wild tips alike for a real lead.

"I will double the current reward we've offered," Zion called out. "I won't rest until we have justice for our daughter."

Ana cringed at the announcement. Beside her Dana and Julia gasped. Laney must have been expecting it, she didn't react at all. Adding to the multi-million dollar reward would only result in more *false* leads for the police department to verify or dismiss.

While she sympathized with Laney's new challenges, she had problems and concerns of her own. Like Zion, she cared less about the fallout and more about finding justice for the victims. More than anything, she wanted to help. And she would, she vowed, even if it meant getting sucked back into a treacherous past better buried, if never forgotten.

Yolanda Cole stepped to the podium, dabbing moisture from her eyes and nose with a tissue. "Services…" Her voice faltered and the sniffle was audible through the microphones.

Ana admired her courage. Up until this point, Zion had done all the talking for the grieving couple.

He wrapped his arm around her shoulders in support. She bit her lip and then took a deep breath. "Sylvia's memorial service will be held Wednesday afternoon at one o'clock at the church." Slowly, she steeled herself, her posture straightening, her head lifting to look out at the crowd of friends and neighbors. "Following the service, we will receive visitors at our home." Another sniffle. "Zion and I would like to express our deep, deep gratitude to everyone for the tremendous support during this difficult time."

Murmurs of sympathy flowed from the crowd toward the Coles as the press conference wrapped up. Ana's gaze tangled with Laney's. Whatever she'd done to get Sylvia's body released, Ana was thankful. Yolanda caught Laney in a big hug before Zion guided her back into the relative privacy of City Hall.

If only Sylvia had been more forthcoming about her relationship with Nolan, the three of them could help each other grieve. Wishing wouldn't fix anything. Never had. Both she and Sylvia had agreed wholeheartedly that actions were far more valuable than ideas and intentions that never got off the ground.

Ana resisted the temptation to seek out Yolanda and check on her. She was on the clinic schedule tomorrow for a follow up on the brief heart-scare that had most likely been grief-induced. Right now, Ana was better off following her intuition. Maybe, if things went well tonight, she would be able to both assist Laney's case and ease Yolanda's broken heart.

CHAPTER FIVE

Ana relaxed on the drive to Troy Duval's house. The weather was clear, though the temperature was dropping as the sun sank into the west. Troy's home, a mansion disguised as a log cabin, sat near the back of his property, affording him the most possible privacy. A respectable vineyard spread out to either side of the long, winding driveway.

The enormous iron gates were closed, as she'd expected. She stopped, rolling down her window. She reached over and pressed the call button on the keypad to let him know she'd arrived.

"I'll open the front door," he said. "Come on in."

She entered her code and waited for the gates to part. Leaving her window down, she breathed in the clean, clear air, soaking up the views and scents of the recently harvested grapes.

At the house, she parked on the left and stepped out of the car. Either Troy or someone he trusted had been working on winterizing his vegetable garden. Who did he trust? She admired his patience and determination with keeping that up, considering his progressing MS. If he didn't already have help, he would need to start interviewing soon.

Belatedly, she noticed his was the only house in the area lacking fall decorations. She didn't claim to have an eye for design, but she could put up a wreath for him. With his permission, of course.

She knocked on the front door and waited a moment before turning the handle and stepping into the foyer. "Troy? It's Dr. Perez."

"In the great room," he called out. "Come on back." His MS limited him almost as much as the tragedy of losing his wife and young daughter to violence. She supposed the quiet restfulness had drawn him to Shutter Lake much as it had her.

"Dr. Perez." He smiled, inviting her to join him near the fire. "This is a nice surprise."

She wasn't so sure he'd think so when she confessed what brought her out to see him. "How are you feeling?"

"Today's been more of a challenge. You understand."

She did. Still, he'd prepared tea. A tray rested on the table between the two chairs closest to the stone fireplace. A cobalt blue tea pot, matching sugar bowl and cream pitcher and two heavy yellow mugs were ready and waiting.

Taking her seat, she let him pour for both of them before she gave him the news. The tea was a warm, spicy chai that soothed the rough edges of her day. "Delicious, thank you."

"You're welcome."

Cupping the tea with both hands, she told him about the press conference. "Sylvia's memorial service is Wednesday afternoon. One o'clock. If you'd like to go I can arrange for —"

He held up a hand, interrupting her. "No need for any special arrangements. I don't plan to attend."

She suspected funerals, especially this one, would be difficult for a man who'd been falsely accused of killing his wife and daughter.

"The Coles are hosting a reception at the house if that would be more comfortable for you," she suggested.

"Dr. Perez—"

"You were more than a client," she said, interrupting him this time. "She spoke quite highly of you and I know she considered you a good friend."

"I merely gave her advice she found useful," Troy replied in the modest manner she considered his trademark. "I may not get out much anymore, but I do still enjoy feeling useful."

Like the property outside, Ana noted his home was neat and cared for. No dust or cobwebs gathering in corners. "How is your new housekeeper working out?"

"I'm not sure." He sipped his tea. "It seems Sylvia is the only one at Sparkle who could tolerate me."

"I'm sure that isn't true."

He arched an eyebrow, a glint of humor in his gaze. "If it gets around that I'm not a grumpy, moldering ogre, I'll have visitors night and day."

This side of him gave her a glimpse into the lively, fulfilled man he'd been. "Whatever your intent, you certainly made a positive impression on Heidi Udall."

"The baker?" He frowned into his tea.

"Yes," Ana confirmed. "That's another reason I stopped in," she said. "She won't be visiting next week as planned. I'm afraid she'll be indisposed for several weeks."

"The drugs caught up with her?"

"You knew about her habit?"

He nodded. "I offered to help her, if she got clean."

Ana digested that. Sylvia had been the first person she'd trusted enough to share snippets of her history. Sylvia had trusted Troy. "Do you know why Heidi started visiting you?"

"I assume someone paid her," he said easily. "Ms. Udall has great potential as an entrepreneur. She lacked focus and strategy. Maybe time in drug rehab will change that."

He didn't sound too confident and Ana had to agree with him. Many users slipped back into the habit despite their best intentions. "Do you have any idea where she bought her drugs? She was less than cooperative when Deputy Chief Holt asked about her dealer. "

"Her dealer doesn't live in Shutter Lake."

"Laney will be relieved to hear it, thank you. Would you like me to continue to stop by as Sylvia did? Not to clean," she joked, "but to visit. I can help with the garden if you like." She hoped she'd still be here to keep any promises to help him in the seasons to come.

He sat back, narrowing his gaze as he studied her. The firelight caressed his face like a lover, and she thought he must have been devastatingly handsome in his prime. "Will you bring sugar-free treats or the real thing?"

Ana laughed. If she'd gone looking for a bright spot in her day, she never would have looked here. It was a refreshing discovery. "I'll bring the real thing," she promised.

And now she had more motivation than ever to make sure she didn't have to run from Shutter Lake like she'd run from the life she'd been born into. There were plenty of doctors who could provide Mr. Duval's care, but the man needed a friend he could count on. So did Ana.

She topped off his tea and hers and settled back into the chair.

"What else is on your mind, Dr. Perez?" He tilted his head toward her hands folded in her lap. "That gesture is your tell that something serious is up for discussion."

She hadn't realized she'd set the mug aside. No sense dawdling over the rest of it now. "You heard they pulled a body from the river yesterday." He always seemed to know a great deal about happenings in town despite keeping to himself out here.

He nodded, though it hadn't been a question. "I assume the body was Josie Rodriguez."

"Yes. They confirmed it earlier."

"Sylvia was convinced that girl was in trouble," Troy said.

"We discussed her concern for Josie a time or two as well." Ana picked up her tea again.

Troy's eyebrows briefly lifted toward his hairline. "What did she tell you?"

"She didn't believe there was any reason for Josie to return to Venezuela. The girl worked part time for Sparkle to help support her parents."

"They relocated to Grass Valley when she was selected for the exchange student opportunity."

Wow. Sylvia had trusted him with more information than Ana anticipated. It bolstered her courage. "What did Sylvia share with you about me?"

"No, no." He waved a hand. "You know that wasn't her habit. In and out of people's homes, her livelihood depended on her discretion. We spoke of Josie's situation simply because she was searching for answers to the girl's disappearance. Whatever she found or learned of a sensitive nature she kept to herself. Gossip would have hurt her business as well as her clients."

He was right. Ana's profession was similar. Sylvia hadn't taken an oath or been subjected to stringent privacy laws, but that didn't make confidentiality less important to a successful career.

"We chatted, of course, about events in town," Troy continued. "But she didn't spread gossip or secrets the way you're implying."

"I don't mean to offend you or her memory. Sylvia's discretion was one of her finest traits. When Josie supposedly flew back to Venezuela and then never checked in, Sylvia grew almost desperate about finding her."

"It bothered her a great deal," Troy agreed.

"As you said, she was convinced the girl was in serious trouble. She was right, clearly. We both assumed the trouble was in Venezuela."

He nodded, his mug balanced on the arm of the chair. "I imagine you were a helpful resource as she planned her trip to South America."

The comment left her momentarily speechless. She might as well be sitting here naked, she felt that exposed. She'd never told Sylvia where she'd been born. She knew her features and coloring were distinctly Hispanic, though she happily let people believe she'd been born in the United States. At this point, it shouldn't matter how or what Troy assumed versus what he knew. From the moment she'd escaped her wicked father and that dreadful life in Colombia, she was living on borrowed time. The security she'd felt in Shutter Lake was as much of an illusion as the woman known as Luciana Perez who became a doctor.

"Sylvia and I discussed how she could stay safe while she

searched for Josie or the family who'd called her back," Ana admitted.

"You gave her a contact, am I right?"

"Were you a psychic before you retired here?"

His gaze drifted to the fire crackling in the hearth. "Unfortunately, no," he replied sadly.

Sympathy swelling, she returned to the subject that only made *her* uncomfortable. "There was no guarantee the contact would be good anymore, but the name and address would have led her to someone helpful. It wasn't smart for her to visit a country on the brink of collapse without some kind of assistance. She refused to let me come along."

"You traveling in that part of the world would've been foolish and you know it."

She had known it. How had he? "For Sylvia I would have risked it." Ana pinned Troy with a long look. "How is it you came to that conclusion?"

"I make it my business to know the people in my sphere. Especially if I need to rely on those people."

Her manufactured background had held up to the city council's extensive checks and verifications. "Are you questioning my credentials?"

"No, not at all." His smile was sincere, if not quite friendly. "Your credentials are solid and your expertise is impressive. I'm delighted you're my doctor."

"However?"

"Relax, Dr. Perez. At this stage of your career, no one else will go looking at your high school transcripts or old mailing addresses unless you give them a reason to do so."

An icy chill slid down her spine. He spoke as if he knew the whole story, as if he'd found the weak link in her manufactured background. The urge to defend herself and to validate her commitment to Shutter Lake, the name and the country she'd adopted was almost irrepressible.

Which was exactly the point, she supposed, taking a breath. He couldn't *know*. He must be baiting her into confirming his suspicions, though she had no idea why. This visit wasn't about her, it was about Sylvia's search for Josie.

"*That* is a good example of why I'm here. The advice and time you gave Sylvia made her a more confident person, which made her even more successful and helped her empower others."

Troy stared her down.

"I'm saying she trusted you as she trusted few others."

He traced the handle of his mug. "I merely emphasized how important it was to know the people around you. Being prepared means avoiding unpleasant surprises."

"I need someone to trust," she said baldly. "Someone to hear me out."

He gestured for her to continue. "Consider this a vault. I want Sylvia's killer found and brought to justice as much as you do."

Ana struggled to sit still as she planned her navigation through a conversation that had become as dangerous as a minefield. One wrong step and Troy would know more than she intended to share with anyone. "When Sylvia was making plans to rescue Josie, she promised me she would create a backup file. It was some sort of golden parachute in case something happened to her during the search."

"You mean a dead man's switch," Troy corrected her. "A golden parachute is a financial term." He leaned forward in his seat. "You've received this file?"

"No. That's what worries me most. She's been dead for days. If no information has appeared anywhere does that mean…"

"Her killer found it and destroyed it." Troy finished the thought.

"Yes. Won't that let the killer escape? Mr. Cole keeps increasing the reward for information and still nothing helpful has come out."

"What is it you know, Dr. Perez?"

"Not enough. Sylvia wouldn't stop digging for answers." Ana sighed, wishing they'd found those answers. "Sylvia came to me weeks ago, absolutely certain she'd seen Josie on an internet porn site. That wasn't her habit, so it had to be something she saw in a client's home."

Troy nodded, attentive.

She felt silly spelling out the way she and Sylvia had attempted to investigate, gathering evidence and fitting together pieces of the puzzle to find the missing girl. "One of her clients recently sought treatment through the clinic for a porn addiction. Another client used to run an adult film company. I don't believe either client was capable of murder or even kidnapping."

"People are capable of dreadful things."

"I know." Ana pinched the bridge of her nose. "I know firsthand the dreadful things people can do. I was drawn to medicine to help and heal, to improve lives."

"And you do."

She waved aside the compliment. "The point is now I am certain that whoever put Josie in jeopardy wasn't in Venezuela. Instead, someone local is killing and kidnapping. Someone who must be my patient."

"You cannot expect to know the minds of everyone you treat," he said gently.

"No." Logically, she understood that. She rubbed her temples. "I read the coroner's report. Sylvia was strangled in her home, by someone facing her."

"Hardly access she'd grant to a random passerby," Troy observed.

"I agree." Ana stood up, too restless to sit still anymore. "I've searched my records and so far, no likely suspect has popped out at me."

"You're not an investigator," he said. "You should take your concerns to Deputy Chief Holt or the chief himself."

"I know." Oh, she knew he was right. "Even if I did that, I can't legally turn over the medical records for all the men in town."

"I suppose it's too soon to have any idea about the build of the person who kidnapped Josie."

"It is. Though the million-dollar reward posted by Quentin Windermere should help."

Troy scowled. "He feels guilty."

"Apparently." She returned to her chair, hoping to bring her spinning thoughts into order. "Considering the millions more Zion is offering for information, anyone who could help should have come forward by now."

Troy stared into the fire for long moments before meeting her gaze. "You don't think Josie was ever in Venezuela."

"Of course not. The flight and ticket must have been a ruse. Sylvia and Josie were close. They talked about everything from mascara to business plans. Sylvia was friendly and approachable. People liked talking to her, even the high school kids. She was young and pretty and a self-made, local success story. Most of them wanted to be her."

He nodded a faint smile shifting the creases on his weathered face. "She was remarkable."

"You know how protective Sylvia could be. When she first heard the women on her staff talking about a girl who'd disappeared from Josie's school in Venezuela it got her attention."

"She had a low tolerance for people being exploited," Troy murmured. "She didn't like to see anyone suffer, especially not those who were working to improve themselves and their situation."

Ana thought that was a fitting eulogy for Sylvia and words that would comfort Yolanda.

"When Sylvia talked to me, she said Josie had heard about the exchange program at school. One of her friends had come to Shutter Lake three semesters ago, hosted by the Windermeres. While she was here, one of their classmates went missing in Venezuela. Runaway they said, but Josie was sure that wasn't the case. In the wake of the missing girl, Josie's parents pushed harder for her to apply to the program. They wanted to give her at least a temporary way out of an increasingly unstable country."

"Sylvia was helping Josie and her parents so they could stay in America."

"Yes," Ana said. "It should have had a happy ending."

"Why didn't it?"

Ana pressed her lips together until the urge to cry passed. "Troy, whatever Sylvia learned about her clients, I don't think that's what got her killed. After hearing the story of Josie's friend I started digging a little. I thought to persuade an old friend to inquire about

Josie's classmate." Her stomach cramped painfully to classify any of the people who'd assisted her father's criminal operation as friends.

"Why?"

"Because it was the right thing to do."

"Did you learn anything helpful?" he queried.

She shook her head. "There was no response." And that had been worse. "In my experience…" She had to stop when her voice broke. "In my experience when good girls disappear from good neighborhoods and happy families they don't go willingly."

"Should I assume you have intimate knowledge of what Josie's classmate might have faced if she was indeed kidnapped?"

"Yes." Ana rolled her shoulders back, ready to deliver the rehearsed reply. "During my time as an attending in ER and in my residency, I treated several victims of trafficking."

The look he leveled on her burned straight to her soul, but she wouldn't speak of her childhood horrors. There was trust and then there was foolhardy. She'd been foolhardy one time too many when she'd contacted one of her father's former cohorts. She'd never forgive herself if her query had led his lieutenants to Josie, if they'd taken that poor girl to quell a potential legal tangle and to send Ana a message.

But if Sylvia had been murdered for her attempts to find Josie and she knew her killer, that meant someone in town was tied to the Rojas trafficking operation. Ana rubbed at her temples again, resisting the obvious, and deadly, logic.

"If you tell the police about the friend you contacted in an attempt to help, I assume you risk exposing your real identity."

Troy understood too well. He might not have the full answers, but he understood. It lifted a weight from her shoulders. "Not everyone in town values discretion, not to mention the legal consequences," she confessed. "I must sound horribly selfish."

"No. Everyone has a past," Troy said, his voice laced with sadness. "Only you can decide if and when taking that risk is the right thing to do. Take time to think it through."

Plus she needed to create an opening to run. She really didn't want to test whether or not Laney would choose friendship and reputation over the law. Did it matter if she passed the citizenship test if she'd done it with false papers? Everything she had now was because of her refusal to fail and her devotion to hard work, but it was all built on the lie of Luciana Camille Perez of El Paso, Texas.

"The more I think about it, the more I fear the killer will escape." Ana tapped her fingertips on her thigh. "If they had solid evidence from Sylvia's house they would have made an arrest already. Any helpful evidence on Josie has surely been washed away by the river."

"I'd think the bigger question is where Josie was kept between the time she disappeared and the time she was found," Troy said quietly, his gaze on the fire again.

She thought of the porn addict and the young, drugged girl the man had seen who resembled Josie. The porn site had been labeled as Viva Venezuela, but the girl could have been held anywhere in the world.

Without her permission, Ana's mind yanked her right back to that dank basement where the dirt floor absorbed the soft sounds of weeping and the harsh scrape of chains and iron cuffs.

Unlike her, Sylvia would never have kept quiet if she'd found a woman being held against her will.

"Dr. Perez?"

"My apologies," she said. "Do you have any ideas about where Sylvia might have stashed her dead man's switch?"

Troy shook his head. "Maybe your worry is for nothing and the police already have it."

"She wouldn't have left it at her house," Ana argued. That didn't mean they couldn't have found it at her office or through a cloud account. "Let's hope that's the case and it leads them to her killer." She stood up and placed her mug on the tray. "I've surely overstayed my welcome. Can I clean this up for you?"

"No, no. I'd rather take care of it on my own." His positive attitude and independence made her job easier and made a world of difference to counter the effects of his disease.

"All right. Thank you for listening." She bent and gave his hand a gentle squeeze. "Deputy Chief Holt will appreciate your reassurance about Heidi's drug dealer."

"Happy to help. Whatever you decide, Dr. Perez, keep in mind how valuable you are to all of us in Shutter Lake."

The last light had long since faded by the time she walked out of the house. As she drove through the vineyard toward the road, she couldn't figure out if she felt better or worse for the time spent with Troy.

Better, she decided, as the gates closed behind her car. At least she'd gotten one answer that would put Laney's mind at ease about the drug situation in Shutter Lake. She headed back into town to share the news with her friend.

Ana stood out on her deck, a thick cable sweater wrapped around her, and a glass of wine in her hand. She gazed up at the stars sparkling in the dark velvet sky as she unpacked every nuance of her conversation with Troy. He'd been subtle, but she'd heard his opinion loud and clear. He didn't want her to risk her position by exposing her own secrets in the search for justice for Sylvia and Josie.

Everyone had an agenda. In Troy's case she didn't think it was completely selfish. There were plenty of qualified doctors the city council could bring in if she did choose to run.

Did she really want to run again? At forty, in a connected world, it wouldn't be as easy as it had been at fourteen. Documentation and security had evolved. Was there a place removed enough for her to practice medicine without her identity being challenged?

Wherever she went next, it wouldn't be anything like Shutter Lake.

The night held a chill, promising frost in the morning. Her little corner of the world seemed so still, as if waiting. Much as she was waiting for inspiration or courage. She wondered which would strike first.

Ana hadn't expected Troy to be so candid. Or to have any idea she hadn't always been Luciana Camille Perez. While that had been disconcerting, she didn't believe he would use those suspicions against her. Troy was clever and emotionally wounded but he clearly held Sylvia in high regard, as did she.

She believed him that he had not been privy to where Sylvia might have hidden or stored the dead man's switch. She did hope he came up with a few ideas because she was fresh out.

It wasn't as if she could walk through Sylvia's home and office, turning over tables and peeking behind the artwork hoping to find a note or flash drive or something. She could hardly tell Laney the 'in case I die' notice she'd been expecting from her friend hadn't yet come through. She didn't want to face the tough questions Laney would ask until she was thoroughly prepared for the fallout.

Ana had spent ten days grieving, distracted and, as the community unraveled, concerned that she would be forced to run or be the next to die.

Listening to the night sounds, she heard an owl in the woods, staking out hunting territory. Creatures rustled in the underbrush. Probably the raccoon or opossum that had tripped her alarm last night.

She rolled the wine glass between her palms. When she told the truth about what she and Sylvia were working on, she had to have her answers ready. Not rehearsed, but locked down, no wiggle room. She would need to be able to give an answer without volunteering the details that would give away her true origins. Laney was a seasoned detective for all that she'd left L.A. behind. McCabe's drinking didn't make him as slow as it might appear after duty. The man was sharp, doubly so when he was on the clock.

Or she could just tell the truth.

Laney and Griff were as compassionate as they were dedicated. It was possible they'd listen to her entire story before calling the immigration office to have her deported.

She heard two quick reports, shredding the tranquility of the night. Not natural sounds. Before her brain registered the sounds as gunfire, pieces of her deck railing splintered. In reflex, she rolled out of the chair, crawling for the door and the safety of her house. A third gunshot shattered her glass door. She jerked away from the danger, cowering in the shadows and wishing she had her phone to call 911. It would be okay. The broken glass would alert the alarm company and help would be here soon.

Ana huddled in that darkness, afraid to move. Waiting. Minutes or hours, time became irrelevant as she braced for the worst. Adrenaline flooded her bloodstream and heightened her senses. Fight or flight? Her mind flickered between past and present terrors. The safest option was to hold still. With light from the house splashing across the deck, any motion gave the shooter a target.

She thought she heard the sound of someone rushing through the woods and couldn't tell if the threat was coming closer or fading away. Would the shooter rush in to finish the job? Hearing an engine on the road out front, cruising by her house and toward town, she hoped it was the shooter fleeing.

Of all the things she'd survived it would be a shame to be killed here and now when she'd been so sure she'd found the safest place on earth.

Her legs cramped, her aching knees were begging for a break. She ignored the small pains. Any discomfort was better than dying. Time passed—she couldn't say how much—and eventually, in quaking, incremental movements, she uncoiled. Breathing easier, she stuck to the shadows as she crept around the house rather than advertising her position by stepping into light glaring like a beacon from the lamp in the living room.

She didn't have her phone or a weapon, but she wasn't defenseless. Improvisation could be as much of an asset as an intentional weapon. By feel she found the hide-a-key in the dark near the garage door and let herself inside. The security panel chirped and she silenced it with the emergency code. If the system worked as advertised, someone from the police department would arrive—silently—in less than two minutes.

Except this was Shutter Lake and response times varied depending on who was on duty. Going to her toolbox, she opened it and grabbed the hammer. Hefting it in her hand, squeezing the grip, she ran through the incident in her mind, searching for any helpful details she could give to the responding officer.

To her surprise, Laney's voice accompanied the sound of a vehicle out front. The deputy chief called out to Ana. A wave of relief and gratitude stalled in Ana's throat. "Here." The word came out as an awkward croak.

"I'll take a look around back." That was Griff's voice.

Ana hurried toward the door as he passed by. "Here," she said, stronger now. She opened the door and turned on the overhead light.

"Holt!" Griff shouted. "I've got her."

He didn't smell like beer or whiskey or the mints from The Rabbit Hole. "Thank you," she said.

Laney appeared, skidding to a stop. "What the hell happened to you?"

Griff started issuing orders and as the words floated over Ana's head, she realized she was sliding into shock. Griff touched her shoulder, urged her to lean on him as he pried the hammer from her grasp.

A red stain marred the wooden handle. "Is that blood?" she asked.

"Yours I think," he confirmed in that steady way he had. "Laney is going to take you to the clinic now."

"I'll wash it." She looked at her hand and flexed it. She couldn't really feel it. "I'm fine."

"Of course you are," Laney agreed, too kindly. "We just need to clean you up."

"There's a first aid kit here." Ana tried to turn, only to have Laney guide her in the opposite direction. "Kitchen."

Griff said something more to Laney as they walked away. Ana couldn't hear the words over the buzzing in her ears. It felt as if her head had been packed with gauze.

"Gunshot from the woods," she said as Laney helped with the seatbelt.

"Okay. We'll figure it out."

"Car," she added, her head lolling back on the headrest.

"Okay. You'll tell me all about it when you're cleaned up."

Ana didn't fight the fog swirling through her mind. It muted the pain pulsing in her hand and the stinging on her cheek. Through the haze, she heard Laney's voice, alternating cadences of command and comfort. She assumed the comfort was aimed at her.

The sensation was as nice as it was foreign, so she let it swallow her.

CHAPTER SIX

Laney's attention was divided between relaying orders through the station, Ana, and driving. Fortunately the clinic was close. Officer Lott Delaney had the overnight shift. What a night to be on, she thought. He'd taken the original alarm call from Ana's security company and now he was juggling orders from Laney and Griff.

"The clinic is ready for her," he said through the radio in the car. "Is she—?"

"I'm just transport," Laney snapped as she turned off Olive Tree Lane toward town. Ana's head rolled back and Laney braced her friend's shoulder through the turn. Suddenly the short drive felt like a cross-country trek. McCabe should've called for an ambulance. The fire department surely would have been able to do more than watch and worry.

Laney felt the sweat beading at her hairline, at her nape under her ponytail. She'd just returned from a long run when the call came through from the station about the alarm at Ana's house. She'd grabbed her badge and gun and headed out.

Laney slammed her car to a stop at the clinic door and hurried around to the passenger side. Donovan Keller, the newest member of Ana's staff, rushed forward with a wheelchair. Lean and lanky, in his late twenties, she could almost hear the click as he snapped into assessment mode.

"What do you know?" he asked, easing his boss into the wheelchair. She roused a little, mumbling something they couldn't make out.

"Not much," she replied. "Only minor injuries are visible. Shock definitely. She mentioned a gunshot and then dropped off on the way over."

"Any other blood?" Keller asked, wheeling Ana through the front door and straight back to the urgent care room, complete with a hospital bed, and state of the art diagnostic tools.

"Only what you see." Laney's stomach pitched. Just a few hours ago Ana had been at the station with the tip about Heidi's cocaine supplier. That moment of relief seemed a lifetime ago now. "Should I call someone?"

Keller was trying to rouse Ana. "Get in here and assist."

"Oh, um." Give her a crime scene over a medical crisis any day. She started to reach for her phone to call the paramedics over from the fire department when he cut away Ana's sweater. Laney cringed and Keller swore.

Most of Ana's injuries seemed to be along her right side. To Laney's untrained eye it looked as if someone had loaded a shotgun with wood chips and fired point blank. The sweater had been little defense against countless splinters imbedded in her skin. Her right hand, cheek, and neck bore the most damage and there were smaller scrapes and scratches.

Blood dripped slowly from the open cuts and deeper wounds. Laney glanced back, seeing the trail of red splotches on the floor, knowing it led right back to her car.

Ana had said gunshot. Was this an accident from a hunter in the woods behind her house? Laney would much rather be out processing the scene with McCabe than here.

"Deputy Chief Holt," Keller snapped. "You're here. I need your help."

It was the tone of command that caught her attention. "Right." She stepped up beside him. "Tell me what to do."

He guided her through finding and assisting with supplies as he started an IV for fluids and a painkiller. He expressed concern about her disorientation and it took Laney several moments to realize he'd activated a voice recorder in the room. The similarity to a coroner's office procedure created a lump of dread in her gut.

Minute by minute she followed Keller's instructions as he treated Ana. He cut away all but her bra and panties. He cleaned up her injuries splinter by splinter, washing away blood and applying bandages or stitches where required. After checking her abdomen and giving her left knee a thorough assessment, he declared the next steps were rest and observation.

He ended the recording and covered Ana with a gown and a warm blanket, dimming the lights as they stepped into the hallway. "You don't have any more information about how she got hurt?"

Laney shook her head, frustrated. Helpless didn't sit well with her. "Chief McCabe and Officer Trask will collect any evidence. Hopefully she'll have more to say when she wakes up."

"No visible head injuries," Keller said, mostly to himself.

"Should you do an MRI or something to be sure? Why is she so loopy?"

"Shock. Her body temperature was a bit low, so she must have been out there a long time. I'll monitor her for a concussion through the night." He shrugged a shoulder. "In the morning she'll tell me it was overkill, but I'm not taking any chances with her."

"Thanks." Laney checked her phone, saw the text message from McCabe that he was staying to secure the property. He'd found one bullet buried in the brick of her fireplace and suspected at least two more were out there. They'd have to wait for the better light of morning.

She was primarily grateful he'd been sober enough to drive himself to the scene. Had the chief finally decided to dry out? He'd certainly chosen the right time, in Laney's opinion.

"I'll stay too," she told Donovan. With two women dead already and another man missing, she didn't feel confident labeling this as an accident or coincidence. "I'll move my car to the parking lot and be right back." Whoever had fired that gun at Ana wasn't going to get another easy shot.

When she entered the clinic again, she had Keller lock the door behind her and then she made sure the two emergency exits were secure.

"You can have the bed," he said.

Ick. "No, thanks. I make it a rule not to sleep in a hospital bed unless I'm a patient."

He laughed. "The overnight suite here is the best staff bedroom I've ever seen."

He gave her a quick tour, but still Laney declined. "You take the bed." She dragged a chair from the waiting room down the hall, right up to Ana's door. "I'll keep watch."

CHAPTER SEVEN

Tuesday October 16

Ana came awake in a rush, immediately aware she wasn't at home. The muted light, clinical smells and soft beeps of monitors gave her little comfort. She remembered the gunshots, the hiding. Remembered Griff and Laney asking questions and her struggle to give them answers. Had they taken her to the hospital?

Cautious, she sat up in the bed, relieved to recognize the décor. She was in one of the two exam rooms the clinic outfitted as full hospital rooms for patients in need of observation or extended immediate care. She took inventory of the bandages on her hand and arm, the tightness in her face and neck that indicated other small wounds and the familiar throb in her knee that occurred whenever she pushed the range of motion.

Based on the jumble of images in her mind, she supposed observation had been called for. Closing her eyes, she tried to put the pieces in the right order. Gunfire and a burst of pain had been followed by abject fear of her past crashing down to destroy her present. She'd always thought she'd be strong enough to resist, to fight. Instead, she'd curled in on herself and willed the crisis to end.

Laney would ask tough questions today and she deserved complete answers. Despite Troy's advice, Ana wasn't sure she could do this without giving up the full truth of her past.

The door opened and Donovan strode in. "Good morning, Dr. Perez. How are you feeling?"

"Better." She tried to smile. "Mostly embarrassed that a few splinters sent me into shock."

He aimed an amused glance her way as he checked the information on the monitors and IV. "Being shot at is probably more intense than say, a picnic."

Snark 101. Her newest P.A. was a master. The younger patients in their care adored him. "What's my prognosis?" she asked.

"You'll live." He winked. "Keep the stitches in your palm clean and dry. One of us can take those out for you next week."

She looked at the bandage across the base of her hand.

"You can peek at it later," he said. Donovan checked her pulse and her eyes. He listened to her heart and lungs and then removed her IV. "You gave Holt a serious scare by passing out on her. Any other complaints or concerns I should know about before I declare you fit for duty?"

Her body ached, her knee especially. Would she ever know how long she cowered in that dark corner of her deck? "Nothing special."

"You were in shock."

"As you said, gunfire is no picnic. I'm sorry I freaked out over a mishap. Thankfully, I had excellent care to get me through. I'm glad you were here, Donovan."

"The flattery's a nice touch, but I'm no pushover." He looped his stethoscope around his neck. "Holt spent the night guarding your door. What else is going on?"

Guarding or waiting for Ana to be alert enough for an interrogation?

"You gave me a scare," Donovan admitted. "Coming in all loopy and muttering nonsense."

What had she said? "Over splinters. That won't do my reputation any good." The IV removed, she tossed back the blanket, belatedly realizing she was in a hospital gown. "You cut off my clothing?"

He narrowed his gaze. "I did a *professional* exam. Your obvious injuries didn't add up to the disorientation. Although you'd clearly been outside without the right gear for a long time, I didn't think it was all caused by the exposure."

She held up her hands in surrender. "Fair enough. You're right." The hospital would have done the same thing, likely without the ideal bedside manner. "Did you run an MRI?"

"You didn't show signs of concussion." He studied her another long moment. "I was waiting to see when and how you woke up today." He rapped his knuckles lightly on the bed rail, giving her time to respond. "All righty. Whatever happened out there isn't my business," he said after a few loaded beats of silence. He crossed to the cabinet and pulled out scrubs for her to wear.

"Thanks." The clock next to the door showed the clinic would open for patients in about an hour. "I'll clean up and be ready for the first patients on time."

"No worries. We've got you covered."

Ana groaned. "Don't tell me everyone knows a few splinters sent me into shock?"

Donovan's gaze filled with more compassion than she deserved. She preferred the snark.

"No," he said at last. "I only planned to let today's staff know you had a rough night."

"Thank you, Donovan. I mean it. I'm glad you were on call."

"Save it for when you see a mirror," he said, a twinkle in his eyes. "If you're not ready to deal with questions, I can tell Laney to go."

"I'll be fine." One way or another. Her escape routes weren't as polished as she would like, but she'd shifted her funds around to make an escape possible.

And if they send you back?

She wished there was a mute button or even a cure for that

annoying voice in her head. Of course, a cure for an internal conscience would open the door for her to become as ruthless as her father and his monstrous associates.

Dressed in the scrubs, she opened the door to find Laney exactly where Donovan had said she'd be. "You stayed all night?"

"Keller roped me into assisting with splinter removal, so I was here. Then McCabe found a bullet buried in your fireplace. After that, staying seemed prudent."

The shot that had taken out the glass door. "Thank you."

"Do you feel up to giving me a statement?"

Clearly, events were escalating. To keep silent only gave the killer more room. "I just need a moment to freshen up, if you don't mind waiting in here."

"What? You don't want an armed cop sitting in the hallway?"

"Even in plain clothes I think it sends the wrong message."

To her credit, Laney grinned and grabbed a tote bag before joining Ana in the room. "You're irritated now, but you'll love me in a second." She dropped the tote on the bed. "I asked Dana to stop by your place and pack a bag for you."

Tears stung the back of her eyes at the kindness and she quickly ducked into the bathroom. The idea of having Dana in her home was like a splash of cold water, snapping her thoughts back into focus. Thank goodness she wasn't in the habit of leaving incriminating documents lying about.

She covered her bandaged hand and stepped under the spray of the shower. Leaving her friends would be the worst, when she did run. She didn't trust easily, for good reason. Lonely was always better than vulnerable and exposed.

Turning off the taps and toweling dry, she couldn't avoid the mirror any longer. Donovan had done good work, though it was startling to face the damage. She imagined it had looked quite a mess last night.

There would be some mild bruising around her eyebrow and cheek. The scratches on her jaw would be the first to heal and the easiest to cover. Patients or no patients, she wondered, turning her face from side to side.

Donovan and the team could cover for her without much inconvenience or worry. She could review the patient load and decide after her visit with Laney.

Combing the tangles from her hair, she managed to get it pulled back into the long ponytail she preferred for office hours.

Emerging from the bathroom, she found Laney dozing in the big recliner near the window. It was tempting to let her rest, though it only delayed the inevitable.

As she was zipping her tote closed, Laney woke. "You're speedy," she noted.

"Medical school," she explained, easing to the side of the bed. Her knee could use a brace and some extra care over the next few days.

"Sore?"

"A little," she admitted. "Mostly stiff. It will loosen up as I get into the day."

"You've never mentioned how you injured it."

"It was dumb luck. I tripped and fell in a stairwell when I was a kid."

It was mostly true. Her father had stomped on the knee when he caught her giving ibuprofen to one of the girls who'd been beaten by a client. He'd issued an ultimatum: she could either join their ranks or haul herself up the stairs. She'd made it out, barely, and he rewarded her tenacity by forcing her to work in his office until she could walk normally again.

She swallowed the familiar, bitter hate and offered up an apologetic prayer to her childhood priest. All these years later and she still hadn't found forgiveness.

"Ana? You okay?"

"Yes, yes." She shoved the memories back into the box where they belonged and shied away from the concern in Laney's gaze. "How can I help?"

"Let's start with what you remember about last night."

She could do this. "After I dropped by the station, I went home to unwind. I was out on the deck, thinking, sipping a glass of wine.

Feeling melancholy I suppose after the confirmation about Josie and announcement of Sylvia's services."

When she paused, Laney only waited, patiently.

"There was some noise. An owl called." She took a deep breath. "Then the gunshots."

Laney sat forward. "Plural?"

"Yes." Surely they knew that by now. "Three."

"You're sure?"

She closed her eyes, thinking it through again. "Yes. The first shot hit the deck railing. The noise, my first thought was gunfire, but when the deck rail flew apart I knew for sure. The next shot followed quickly. I moved toward the house and then the glass door exploded in front of me."

"Three shots," Laney echoed. "Nothing more?"

"Three shots, yes," Ana confirmed.

"How do you know what gunfire sounds like?"

Ana paused, swallowed the uncharacteristic urge to snap at her friend. "There have been hunters out there before."

"And no prior mishaps with bullets finding your house rather than the wildlife?"

"No."

Laney's head bobbed slowly. "One misfire I understand, not three."

"I agree," Ana said. "I took cover in the corner of the deck, cursing myself for leaving my phone inside."

"Can you think of any reason someone might be firing a gun at you?"

Two. At least. Recalling Troy's advice, she gave Laney the most likely reason. "The person who killed Sylvia may see me as a threat as well."

"You know who killed Sylvia Cole?"

"Of course not." Ana bristled. "I would never have kept that to myself."

"Sylvia was strangled."

"Yes. Most likely by a known assailant." Ana met and held Laney's gaze. "I read the report."

"Me too. Repeat killers usually stick with one method."

Ana nearly argued, having seen killers use whatever was at hand to dispose of unwanted witnesses or underperformers. It took a moment for her to quiet her thoughts and gather her composure.

"Sylvia and I believed someone in Shutter Lake lured Josie away with the intent to use or harm her. We may have rattled the wrong cages in our effort to find the girl and a possible connection to other missing teens."

Laney sat forward. "Why not make a report?"

"At the time, she and I were the only two people who believed Josie was missing. Her parents hadn't heard from her, but communications in Venezuela are sketchy."

"You should have come to me or Griff."

"And how would you have proceeded on our flimsy concerns or suppositions?" Ana's temper was fraying around the edges. "There wasn't enough to file a formal report. We didn't have names or even a hard trail to follow. We had a story that didn't quite add up and a young girl whose parents were in need of the utmost discretion."

Laney subsided, drumming her palms on her thighs. "I've met Josie's parents. Sylvia made sure their paperwork is in order." She pursed her lips. "Are you trying to tell me you think the shooting last night was a coincidence?"

"No."

"So three gunshots and you wisely took cover. When did you decide it was safe to move?"

Ana massaged her left knee before she could stop herself. "I waited and waited, refusing to give the shooter a target. I heard a car on the road out front and eventually went to call for help."

"You didn't go inside?" Laney queried.

"That would have put me in the light."

"True," Laney agreed.

"And the glass." She twisted her wrist, flashing the bandage. "My hand was throbbing and I didn't want to crawl through it, so I went around to the garage where there would be something I could use for a weapon in case I hadn't waited long enough."

"You picked up a hammer," Laney said absently. "And you have no idea how long that was."

It wasn't a question, so Ana didn't reply.

"The alarm from your security company came through just after midnight." She flicked the tab on the front zipper of her running jacket.

Ana must have cowered for nearly two hours, risking her health in the cold October night. No wonder her knee ached like the devil himself held it in a vicious grip.

"How long?" Laney pressed.

Ana shrugged. "Two hours? I went out around ten, before bed."

"Two hours? You left a blood trail from my car to the exam room."

"Slices and scrapes of the face and hands are like that." She prodded the bandage on her hand. "This one likely would have opened again when I moved to the garage."

"You'd know all of that better than me."

"Has anyone else mentioned hearing a car?" Ana queried.

"We'll ask around today. As you know, homes on Olive Tree Lane are a bit spread out, so the odds are low."

Privacy was one of the perks of that area. Ana's closest neighbor was dead. It still bothered her that she hadn't heard anything out of the ordinary the night Sylvia had died.

"Tell me more about what you and Sylvia were digging up in your search for Josie."

"Sylvia's line of work gave her unusual access and insight into her clients." She checked Laney's reaction, but the woman might as well be playing championship poker. "Josie said she'd been called back to Venezuela. Sylvia didn't like it, for Josie's sake. Then a few days later Sylvia came to me, thinking she'd found evidence Josie was being exploited in Venezuela."

"Where did she find that evidence?"

"In a client's home," Ana replied. "She didn't tell me which client." The dots had been connected a few days ago when Wade Travis lost his teaching job and entered a program to treat his pornography addiction. "When she explained her concern, she admitted she wasn't sure the young woman was Josie, but the discovery lit a fire under her to find the girl."

"And Sylvia involved you because?" Laney pressed.

It wasn't the question she was expecting, or the one she was fully prepared to answer yet. In her mind, Troy's voice reminded her of the high stakes. "We are—were—good friends. Sylvia trusted me to be discreet."

"*Mm-hm.*" Laney shifted, her gaze sharpening. "Ana, did she force you to help her somehow?"

"What?"

"I think you know what I'm asking. Did your good *friend* give you an ultimatum? Help her or else?"

Ana gaped, not at all sure of the best reply. "Or else? No. Sylvia wasn't that way."

An odd disappointment washed the intensity from Laney's features. "All right. I'm going home to sleep for a couple of hours." Clearly exhausted, she braced her hands on her knees as she stood up. "McCabe will follow up with you this afternoon. Hopefully he'll have some evidence that will help us find the shooter."

"Laney wait," Ana stood as well, her hands clasped at her waist. "Sylvia only came to me rather than the police when she thought Josie was in trouble because I had more knowledge of how women get exploited."

"How did you come by that knowledge?"

"Medical school residencies." It wasn't a complete fabrication. Her residencies had bumped up against drug and human trafficking along with plenty of prostitution-induced injuries and illnesses.

"And you didn't come to me with this." Laney's eyes were hard, accusing. All the earlier sympathy had drained away. "Zion Cole has been throwing money at a reward and you kept this information to yourself. Why not cash in?"

"Because I don't *know* anything." She shook out her hands, frustrated with herself and Laney and Sylvia's secrets. "I—we—planned to bring you something concrete, but we only had wispy rumors. Sylvia was murdered before we had anything substantial enough to call proof."

Laney stalked back into the room, stopping at the opposite side of the bed, her hands gripping the rail hard. "You had enough to feel fine about sending Sylvia to Venezuela to find Josie?"

"No, we didn't. I urged her not to go." Ana's palms were damp as she realized the magnitude of her error. "I swear, Laney, I wanted to bring you in earlier."

"You lectured *me* about giving Yolanda Cole closure while you were sitting on something helpful to the investigation. What you know might have led us to the killer."

"But I wasn't sitting on anything," Ana protested. "It's not like that. I don't—"

"Stop." Laney held up her hands. "Just. Stop. I'm too exhausted for this. I won't haul you out of here in cuffs, but you will come to the police station when the clinic closes today and tell McCabe and me everything you know. And you'll bring all your notes and documentation, whatever you have."

Ana nodded, protests and excuses and apologies clogging her throat. Pointing out that she didn't have notes or documentation would only land on deaf ears.

"If you try to dodge this, Dr. Perez, I will arrest you and charge you with obstruction of justice." She turned on her heel and stalked out of the room leaving Ana to wallow in the mess she had created.

CHAPTER EIGHT

Ana would have preferred to go home, to hide, or even to run. She had the personal leave and confidence in her staff to handle the schedule without her. If any of her patients had walked in with the symptoms she'd presented last night, she would have insisted that patient rest today and probably tomorrow.

Instead, Ana got to work.

She couldn't grant herself the same care protocol. Not today. She needed to be here for Yolanda Cole's follow up appointment. Just three weeks ago, Sylvia's mother had been a vivacious and delightful person, so proud of her one and only child. Yolanda embraced life and people with a warm brand of kindness, and went out of her way to make sure others felt valued.

Yolanda had no idea how rare that was.

Approaching the exam room, Laney's accusations of hypocrisy echoed through Ana's mind. Laney was wrong, she told herself. She hadn't pushed for the family's rights while holding back information that would impact the investigation. It bothered her that Laney questioned her integrity as a doctor and as a friend.

She pushed all of that out of her head as she knocked on the exam room door. "Mrs. Cole," she said, stepping inside. "How are you feeling?"

Yolanda, in her late fifties, had taken excellent care of herself, her commitment to both health and fashion holding her in good stead during the worst possible circumstances. Today, the rose-colored sweater over rich brown slacks put color in her face that almost hid the signs of grief and stress. Her normally bright smile was strained and the shadows under her eyes were still pronounced.

"I suppose I'm sleeping a bit better." She lifted her hand toward Ana, as if she wanted to touch the wounds on her face. "What on earth happened to you?" Her gaze dropped to Ana's bandaged hand. "Are you okay?"

"Nothing serious," Ana assured her. "A hunter misfired in the woods last night and caught my deck. Just an awkward accident."

"Someone shot at you?"

"No, no." She couldn't let that kind of rumor get started, especially when it was the truth. "A bullet grazed my deck and the splinters caught me. It looks much worse than it is. We're here to talk about you and how you're coping."

"I'd much rather talk about you." The concern in Yolanda's gaze didn't fade. "I feel so selfish missing Sylvie. I can't seem to think of anything else. Then I'm so tired." She tucked her hair behind her ear. "So I try to nap, but instead I'm just so... empty."

"All of that is perfectly natural. And as we discussed, your symptoms are exacerbated by the challenging circumstances. You need time that's all."

"The memorial will help." She glanced up, her eyes watery as she pressed a hand over her heart. "It has to, right?"

"It will." Ana smiled gently. "Have the sleeping pills helped?"

"Some, thank you. Although you know how I feel about medications."

"That's certainly understandable, but this isn't the time to be stoic or power through. This is the time to take the support you need. It's not forever." She reviewed the intake form on the chart. Yolanda's blood pressure and pulse were a smidge high, but not worrisome, considering the situation. "We all need help from time to time from friends or medicine or both."

"That's true. Oh, Ana, I miss her so much."

"She'd want you to take care of yourself. I was glad to see you out and about on Saturday at the fundraiser for the arts."

"It was a nice afternoon." She dabbed at her eyes. "Several people shared memories of Sylvia. It meant a lot." She reached for a tissue and then fanned her face. "I put on makeup and mascara today so I wouldn't blubber."

"You can blubber in here anytime. What did you have for breakfast today?"

"One of the shakes you recommended."

"Are those helping?"

"They stay down better than that heavy sympathy food the church groups keep bringing over." She clapped a hand to her mouth. "Oh, that sounds rude and ungrateful."

"This is a safe place," Ana reminded her, stifling a chuckle. "Who's catering the gathering after the memorial?"

Yolanda's eyes lit up. "One of Katherine Windermere's favorite chefs from San Francisco. The woman makes a teriyaki beef and broccoli that Sylvia raved about. And the chef was gracious enough to agree to be ready within twenty-four hours since we didn't know when the service would be held.

"Zion wasn't in favor of the reception," she added with a frown. "He's worried it's too much for me and I know he'd rather not have a house full of people, but I just need that connection."

"Of course you do. It's natural to want to add to your memories of Sylvia."

"You keep saying it's natural for me to be so devastated and consumed, but here you are, doing your job. You were one of her best friends. I feel like such a weakling."

"Not at all." Ana couldn't help it, she reached out and covered Yolanda's hands. "You're her mother. Sylvia frequently told me how strong you were. You were her inspiration."

"That's silly. Her father inspired her," Yolanda said, shying from the praise. "Oh, how they butted heads at times," she said with a rusty chuckle.

"Did they?" Curious now, Ana encouraged Yolanda to share. "When?"

"Off and on through the years." Her smile turned wistful. "They were so much alike, those two. Strong wills and stronger minds and both of them too stubborn to give an inch when they made a decision."

Ana smiled. "I bet they were quite a pair."

"I wish Zion would come in and see you too. I might be struggling to eat and sleep, but he's suffering in his own way." She rolled her eyes. "Even I know that ridiculous reward is making it harder to find Sylvia's killer."

"Chief McCabe and the entire department are committed to solving the case."

"I know they are. The reward is Zion's way of making restitution. I think he's feeling guilty. Those last weeks before our Sylvie died the two of them were at odds over something. She wouldn't even stop to eat lunch with me if her father was around."

This was fascinating and troubling news. She and Sylvia had been systematically looking at all of the people in Josie's life. Had Sylvia suspected Zion of some wrongdoing? The day before she'd been killed, she'd confided in Ana that she was closing in on a likely suspect. Concerned the information would get out, she'd refused to go into any detail via text or phone call. Sylvia had been murdered before they could get together to discuss it.

Though Ana wanted to press Yolanda for more information Laney might find helpful, she had to tread carefully for the sake of her patient. "Family meals were important to the three of you," Ana said. "Sylvia told me how you insisted on eating dinner together throughout her childhood."

Yolanda bobbed her chin in vigorous agreement. "I think family dinner is a critical element of giving children a solid foundation. Even when Zion traveled, Sylvie and I ate together at the table. Did you have that with your parents?"

"No, unfortunately. My childhood was a bit rockier than the love and stability you gave Sylvia."

"I am sorry to hear that, Dr. Perez. And so pleased you found your way to a fulfilling career."

"Thank you." She rested her hands on the top of the tablet in her lap. "My reason for bringing up dinner goes back to your trouble with keeping down food. The issue might be related to how vital mealtime was to the three of you. Give yourself time, keep supplementing with the shakes, and maybe change one or two things about dinnertime with Zion to give both of you a fresh start and create a new tradition."

"That's quite smart. I'll give it some thought."

"Good. Your blood pressure is still slightly elevated, but everything else looks normal. I'd recommend taking a walk in the sunshine once a day. You have gorgeous views on the property this time of year. You might have more success napping after that."

"That's what I did when Sylvia was a baby," Yolanda said. "She'd soak up the fresh air and sunshine and then she'd drop off for a long nap."

"Sunshine is a proven health booster at any age," Ana said. "I'll plan to see you back in a week, but if you need me sooner, just call or come right in. The team up front has instructions to work you in."

"Thank you, dear." Yolanda cradled Ana's hand gently between her own. "And do take care of yourself. We'd be lost without you around here."

"I promise to be careful." She just couldn't promise to stay.

The clinic hummed along through a morning that was only half as hectic as Monday had been. Ana and her staff dealt with regular check-ups and a variety of minor illnesses and injuries, including the first positive strep test of the season.

An alert for strep went up on the board in the staff room, as well as in the computer system, generating a banner that would pop up on the tablets they used during appointments. If this season followed the pattern of those prior, more cases would come in over the next several days.

'Tis the season, she thought, logging patient notes while she wolfed down half a sandwich and a cup of soup from Stacked at her desk.

Being the primary caregiver for an entire town had solidified Ana's sense of purpose and responsibility and given her great satisfaction. Having the support of city leadership for wellness programs added a unique case study opportunity she wished she could seize.

Early in her life, she'd witnessed a community with zero interest in wellness. In her battered hometown in Colombia, the focus was survival and disease control rather than prevention. Now she was blessed to see the opposite philosophy in action. A healthy lifestyle didn't take that much work once the mindset was in place.

Occasionally during her tenure as Shutter Lake's primary physician, she'd jotted down notes. A couple of times, she'd gone so far as to outline a paper. Though the city might sign off on a publication if their identities were protected, she could never publish. That would be too much pressure on her established identity.

Especially if she had to bolt. Ah, well. Maybe if she left her notes behind Donovan or her replacement could write it and use it to further a career. She couldn't afford the attention that sort of publication would bring.

When the timer on her computer sounded, she cleaned up her lunch and left her office to resume her appointments. In the hallway, she caught a whiff of spice and peppers. The distinct cigar tobacco, aided by the recent events, dragged her back through time.

Heading home from school, she turned into the street, her breasts hot and itchy under the tight binding that hid her changing shape. The discomfort was forgotten when she saw her father, sitting outside, holding court with two men in suits, a thick cigar in hand.

Even from this distance she could smell the rich, acrid scents of the tobacco. Not his usual blend, which could only mean he'd cut a deal.

Panic clawed at her throat. Her feet stopped moving. She'd thought she had more time. Another day or two, at least. A pack was stowed under her bed. When Sergio Rojas prepared to sell his prime women, he often took weeks to negotiate the best price.

She could see by the smug look on his face he'd found the right buyer for her right off the mark.

He'd noticed, despite her efforts to hide her changing body. Her value in his eyes was even higher because she knew the life, had particular knowledge about his system. He would want assurances from the buyer, from her, to ensure his business wouldn't suffer.

Her knowledge had saved her from being sold into the sex trade years earlier, when she could have easily been manipulated into giving up his methods. When her soul would have been crushed long before her body died. She'd been told to be grateful he kept her around, continued to see her fed and educated.

Clearly his generosity had run out.

She took a step backward, away from the only home she'd known. Her first outward act of defiance. He squinted at her through a wreath of smoke. She backed up again.

Shock and disbelief gave her the head start she needed.

She bolted. Ran, but not blindly. Evil as he was, she'd learned from Rojas. She'd planned routes. Created alternates and contingencies.

She didn't stop until she was clear of the neighborhood. She kept running, knowing she would never return and never see her family or friends again. She ran away from the hell she knew too well into the absolute unknown. It surely couldn't be any worse.

Even without the small pack stashed under her bed, she made her first checkpoint. Her teacher's elderly aunt gave her some food and the only cash she had on hand.

Weeks later, hiding in Mexico, she'd learned just how closely Rojas' lieutenants had tailed her. The woman's kindness had been repaid with a slow and merciless death.

CHAPTER NINE

Returning home from the clinic, Yolanda watched the chickens scurry out of her way as she circled the house to the gate at the side yard. Following Dr. Perez's suggestion, she walked on out toward the horse barn, her eyes on the gorgeous view. With nearly a hundred acres it should be easy to forge a path she hadn't shared with Sylvia, but she couldn't find it today.

It seemed every blade of grass or splash of sunlight across the mountainside reminded her of times with her daughter. As a baby and little girl, Sylvia had been fascinated with the animals. Yolanda thought she might pursue a career as a veterinarian. Later, as a young woman, Sylvia shared corners of this vast space with her friends.

Yolanda and Zion had done everything right. They'd worked hard, their efforts and success rewarded tenfold when they joined others and committed to carve out this idyllic paradise. They might still have their fortune and their health, but what did any of it matter without their precious daughter?

She rolled her ankle on a loose clump of dirt near the barn and turned back toward the house. A more serious walk should wait until she was dressed for it. As she approached the house, she stopped short, her breathing ragged as she came face to face with the stone fireplace and wide deck that spanned the back of the house.

Twelve days ago she and Zion had sat right up there while Chief McCabe and Deputy Holt delivered the news that their daughter was dead. She'd avoided the spot ever since.

Twelve days of a bleak hopelessness. It might as well be twelve years.

Denial had been brief and no protection at all against the grief that rolled over her in drowning waves. She could look at the calendar and know it was too soon to expect herself to move on and far too late to go back.

Dr. Perez had asked her how she was feeling today. She wasn't feeling. Not today. Not in the days before. That was the problem. It was as if someone had dialed down the sun, muted the vibrant colors of autumn. There was a vast emptiness she couldn't comprehend filling.

Motherhood had defined her more than she realized. But she was also a wife and her husband was grieving. Their marriage had always been a strong one, their family of three a tightly-woven unit. She couldn't forget that even as he propped her up, he too needed support.

They'd both been a bit baffled when Sylvia rebelled against a traditional college path and leapt right into business ownership. As time moved on, they'd both been proud to see that business grow, to see their daughter's vision and influence expand as she dedicated herself to improving the community as well as her bottom line.

These past twelve days the community was the only thing keeping Yolanda going. If the press conferences were a challenge, the troubling lack of progress in the investigation was worse. Lately though, when she had ventured into town, people would speak highly of her daughter. She soaked up those moments, hoarding them to get through the long, sleepless nights.

Right now, Renata and Lucy, Sylvia's first two employees, were cleaning the house from top to bottom for the gathering that would follow Sylvia's funeral tomorrow. Yolanda should give them room to work, but she couldn't bear to be out here a moment longer. She hurried across the deck and through the French doors into the house, not stopping until she reached the relative safety of the kitchen.

Her heart racing, she poured a glass of water and sipped it slowly.

On the refrigerator a magnet with Sylvia's business card mocked her. Everywhere she looked she saw remnants of the daughter she'd never speak to again.

Sylvia had assembled a unique family of professionals at Sparkle. Yolanda knew they were all grieving, yet the office downtown was one place she still couldn't face. She'd been told Sylvia's house was still protected as a crime scene.

Who would clean that out? Surely the police wouldn't ask the girls from Sparkle to take care of it. No one would be that cruel. Zion likely had a realtor and a service lined up as soon as the police gave the all-clear. She pressed a hand to her stomach. Of course they would need to sell the house across town. After they'd collected the last bits of Sylvia's life and brought them here.

"Mrs. Cole?"

Yolanda jumped at the sound of Renata's voice. Before she turned around, she swiped at her cheeks, a new habit since tears were frequent. "Yes. It's good to see you." She walked over and gave the girl a quick hug. It had to be quick so she wouldn't cling. "Is everything set?"

"Almost." Renata smiled as if she could see Yolanda's struggle. "The office is locked. We can leave it again if you like."

Again? "Oh, but the key should be in the door." She started forward. Zion closed himself in when he was consulting or studying new investment opportunities. He was officially retired but his work ethic wasn't easily ignored.

"Usually, yes. Not today or last week."

Yolanda was ashamed to realize she had no recollection of Renata's visit last week. "Did you ask me, then?" The younger woman nodded. "And I suppose I told you to leave it."

"You did, yes, ma'am." Renata smiled in understanding and sympathy. "This is a difficult time."

"For all of us." Her selfishness embarrassed her. "I apologize."

"You're hurting," Renata replied.

"As are you." Yolanda reached down and found a scrap of courage. "I know how Sylvia valued your friendship. You were the sister she never had. I remember when she was about nine years old…"

Renata's deep brown eyes filled with patience and compassion and something snapped inside Yolanda. She couldn't finish the story. Couldn't force Sylvia's dear friend to be her emotional crutch.

"Oh, forgive me," she said instead. "You've heard all the stories. I'm sure Zion will want to keep the office closed tomorrow afternoon anyway." She stared at the closed French doors. The classic skeleton key they kept in the lock was missing. "Two weeks in a row?" She tested the handle. It refused to turn.

"Yes, ma'am."

"How much dust and mess can one man generate in two weeks?"

Renata's expression went carefully blank.

Yolanda laughed, the sound brittle in her ears. "We both know the answer to that." She forced her lips into a smile, hoped it wasn't a grimace. "The man often retreats into his work, as you know."

"We all cope differently."

Yolanda made a decision in that moment. "I'd like you girls to sit with us tomorrow at the service, as family."

Renata's eyes went wide. "Mrs. Cole."

"Sylvia would want you all there as her sisters and it would mean a great deal to us."

Renata sniffled and reached into her pocket for tissue. "I'll tell the others."

A few minutes later, Yolanda was alone in the house again. She wandered upstairs to Sylvia's old room. The room no longer resembled anything of her daughter, arranged now as a guest suite. Sylvia had helped her make the transition, a memory that gave her comfort now. She stroked the velvet upholstery of the slipper chair, sinking down as her knees buckled.

"Oh, baby, I miss you so." She hugged a pillow to her chest. "I wish you'd talked to me those last weeks when you were so angry. It wasn't like you to keep secrets from us."

She wondered if Sparkle had been in financial trouble. Unlikely, but every business went through ups and downs. Zion had drilled that into her head from the first days of their marriage. Yolanda would ask him about it when he got home. If financial trouble was the source of tension between her husband and daughter, he would know how best to protect the employees Sylvia cared for like family.

Dr. Perez had recommended she take a nap this afternoon but she was too restless for sleep, even after the short walk. She fluffed the pillow and put it back on the daybed, feeling as if someone flipped a switch and she suddenly had too much energy.

She wandered the house, wishing Zion would come home. Unless he was in the locked office, he was probably out driving. He'd gone out last night as well. No rhyme or reason to it. Driving soothed him in times of stress almost as much as business.

Early in their marriage, they would often take long drives along the Pacific Coast Highway or little-known backroads, exploring pockets of beauty and interest along the way. It's how they'd discovered the area that would become Shutter Lake.

Yolanda found herself standing at the office door, wondering what Zion was working on that he felt the need to lock her out. She rattled the handle, more from worry than any real desire to get inside. The door swung open and she somewhat stumbled over the threshold.

When her husband looked up, the harsh expression on his face startled her. His blue eyes were like shards of ice and the malice she saw there frightened her. Then he blinked and once more, he was the caring man she'd loved for more than half her life. It occurred to her Sylvia would never know that kind of love and romance and a sob caught in her throat.

"Yolanda." He stood and rounded his desk. "Are you all right?"

He reached for her, but she stepped out of reach, flustered. "I didn't mean to interrupt. I was only looking for you."

"Did you need something?"

"No. Not really. I was just lonely," she admitted. "I thought you were out."

He pointed to the door that allowed clients to come and go without walking through the house. "I came in through the back after another visit with McCabe."

She could tell by his voice there hadn't been any more news. No wonder he'd been angry moments ago. He guided her over to a low couch tucked under the window and sat down with her.

"What is it, love?" he asked, stroking the backs of her hands with his thumbs.

"The girls were cleaning for tomorrow. Except in here. The door was locked."

"Does it need to be open to guests tomorrow?"

"Of course not." She smiled weakly, her attention fixated on a bit of lint on her pants. "I told Renata the same thing."

He cradled her hands in his, giving her a reassuring squeeze. "We'll get through."

"We will." Tears threatened. She was so very tired of crying. "Maybe I need a nap after all."

"Maybe so. I worry about you."

His tenderness soothed her and she wanted to do more for him. "What do you need, Zion? We're both grieving."

"Tomorrow will help me," he said immediately. "We might not have her killer in custody, but it will help to know our daughter is properly laid to rest."

"I told Renata that the Sparkle girls should sit with us as part of the family."

"That was thoughtful." His hands stilled. "Sylvia would approve."

She knew he'd understand. "Especially after the news about Josie," Yolanda said. "I'm almost glad Sylvia didn't live to deal with that."

He gave her hands another gentle squeeze. Those hands had

helped her through every facet of life. With her, he'd raised their little girl with compassion and courage. Taught her how to be strong and follow through with her convictions. Those were good hands holding her, supporting her now.

Suddenly the bruises ringing her daughter's neck flashed into her mind. They'd warned her not to look at those pictures. Whose hands had left behind such brutal violence on her baby girl?

Zion tipped up her chin and wiped away the tear on her cheek. "We'll get through, sweetheart," he whispered. "Together."

He pushed to his feet and she missed the warmth of his touch.

"Murder is beyond McCabe's scope," he said. "Twelve days and no valid leads."

"The Bradshaw boy's confession bogged things down," she reminded him. "Deputy Chief Holt has the experience."

Zion grumbled, staring out the window. "I've been researching private detectives," he said suddenly. "Interviewed a few as well. An outsider looking at the case may be our only chance at justice for Sylvia."

"That's where you've been going?"

He nodded. "When I find the right one, you'll know."

"Find the right one soon," she replied. "After what happened to Dr. Perez last night I don't think the killer is done."

Zion scowled down at her. "What are you talking about?"

"Someone fired a gun at Dr. Perez last night. A hunter, she said. She was working today of course. Nothing stops that woman."

"We're fortunate to have her." He sounded unhappy, but his gaze was tender when he reached out and touched her cheek.

She should ask him about Sylvia's business, if that's what had come between them in what had been her final weeks. Surely he regretted that his daughter died before they'd talked things out.

Instead, she leaned in and gave him a long hug. He needed comfort too. Leaving him to his search for a private investigator, she headed upstairs, her mind a tangle of love and loss and more questions than ever.

CHAPTER TEN

Moving between exam rooms, Ana caught sight of Dana's red cap of hair at the reception desk and walked out to greet her friend. "You're well?"

"I'm great," Dana said. "I was worried about you." Her gaze unerringly inventoried Ana's scrapes and bandages.

"It looks worse than it is," Ana assured her, drawing her back toward her office. "Thank you so much for bringing me fresh clothes this morning."

"You're welcome. Do you need anything else?"

A way to repair the damage she'd done to her friendship with Laney, but she wouldn't bring Dana into that. "Not right now." Ana gave her a quick hug, just in case this was the last chance. "Thanks for being a good friend."

Dana studied her a bit too closely for comfort. "Whatever is troubling you, Ana, you know you don't have to cope with it alone."

"I appreciate that." She couldn't accept it, but she appreciated it.

At the end of the day, she allowed one of the medical assistants to change the bandage on her hand just for practice. Then she went to her office under the guise of recording her patient notes and locked the door.

At her desk, she pulled out the center drawer and popped it out of the track. She removed the small plastic bag and tucked it into her purse. It was the first time in years that the short list of names and cell phone numbers was on her person. As prepared as she'd ever be, she walked away from the clinic, hoping she'd be allowed to come back.

She could have driven from the clinic to the police station and might have done so if the weather hadn't been so nice. Additionally, it set a good example for others to have the doctor demonstrating the habits she encouraged. Many a mentor through medical school had encouraged students looking toward general practice to lead by example. Staying fit and healthy not only made it easier to do the job, it lent credibility to the advice given in the exam room.

At the police station, Laney was waiting, her expression hovering closer to cynical than neutral. Ana was primed for an uphill battle. It certainly wouldn't be her first.

"You look rested, Deputy Chief Holt."

"You're on my turf now." Laney's mouth thinned. "This way, Dr. Perez."

Ana had expected the interrogation room. The audio and visual recording equipment was no surprise either. For several minutes Laney sat across from her in utter silence. The approach had surely intimidated many offenders when Laney worked as an LAPD detective.

The tactic posed no problem for Ana. She considered her ability to wait and watch an innate talent. Ana refused to ask if Griff had found any evidence of the shooter near her home. It might not be her home by the end of this interview.

Griff walked in and closed the door. Taking the seat next to Laney, he placed a slim manila folder on the table. Ana wondered who might be watching on the other side of the glass.

Laney turned on the recording equipment and stated the date, time and location. "State your name for the record."

"Luciana Camille Perez."

"You're here as a person of interest regarding the murder of Sylvia Cole," Laney said.

Ana couldn't control her surprise and Laney's carefully composed face made her palms sweat. They couldn't possibly believe she'd killed her friend. She took a deep breath, recalling the coroner's report. The killer was a tall man. "I'm here to cooperate to the best of my ability."

Griff allowed Laney to take the lead. Through the course of several probing questions, she drew out a full statement about Ana's whereabouts on the night of Sylvia's murder.

"What knowledge did you have of Sylvia's sexual relationships?"

"As her doctor, I was aware she had sexual relations."

Griff reached over and stopped the recordings. Laney swore and started to argue. He ignored her, his gaze locked with Ana's. "I have no intention of bringing charges of any type against you, Dr. Perez," he stated. "Barring murder, of course."

"I haven't killed anyone and I have not intentionally obstructed your investigation."

"Then *talk*," Laney demanded. "Help us find the killer."

Ana took a deep breath. "Working in people's homes, Sylvia learned things. She overheard conversations and noticed details. With her staff, she shared a close bond. Her employees would often speak with her quite candidly about anything."

"And?" Laney prompted when Ana paused.

"When Josie started at Sparkle, somehow the discussion of human trafficking came up." She thought back to how she'd explained the issue to Troy and laid out the information in a similar way. "A girl from Josie's school in Venezuela disappeared while a previous classmate was staying here with the Windermeres as an exchange student.

"Sylvia thought that was a weird coincidence," Ana continued. "It's a pervasive problem and she dug into the issue, searching news articles for missing teens from other schools that sent students here."

Griff pinched the bridge of his nose. "She found more?"

"Yes," Ana confirmed. "There was a disturbing correlation between exchange students here in Shutter Lake and other teens going missing in the areas they came from. Most of those who went missing simply disappeared, usually on their way to or from school."

"You have any proof?"

"No. Sylvia kept the documentation to herself." Ana bit back further explanation. Her father had used teams of kidnappers in similar ways. His lieutenants would find the type of girls in demand and, after learning their schedules and patterns, they plucked the girls like ripe fruit.

"How does her research tie to Josie's disappearance?"

Ana laced her fingers in her lap, willing her voice to hold steady. "I am honestly not sure. I also know that none of the previous exchange students who came here were abducted once they went home. It was always someone else... until Josie. Sylvia never believed the family had called Josie back to Venezuela. When she didn't check in, Sylvia got worried. If the girl on the porn website was Josie, then maybe the trafficker meant to silence her or somehow make Sylvia stop nosing around."

Laney's scowl turned ferocious. "You believe someone here in Shutter Lake is trafficking teens?"

"Why else would anyone want to kill Sylvia and Josie?"

"And you," Griff said. He and Laney exchanged a glance. "I'm concerned that you were attacked last night, shortly after stopping by the station."

Before she had a chance to process that detail, Laney tossed out another question.

"When did Sylvia decide to search for Josie in Venezuela? What prompted her to start down that path?"

"One of her clients had a pornography habit," Ana replied. "While cleaning, she found pictures of a girl closely resembling Josie on a site labeled as Viva Venezuela. With the site name matching Josie's home country, she thought it was worth the trip."

"Child porn is a crime," Laney grumbled. "She should've brought this to us,"

"She didn't want the pornography addict she wanted Josie. She grilled her client for information and then she confided in me. She didn't want to worry Josie's parents unnecessarily. I knew the language better than she did and I'd dealt with trafficked victims during my residency and early years as an attending physician so I knew a bit of the system. I had a better idea what to look for."

"Look for?" Griff echoed.

Ana paused. She would be more comfortable walking a tightrope over a canyon. "From what I've learned, traffickers are sneaky by design and extremely cautious. Sylvia was insisting on going to Venezuela alone. I was teaching her how to be alert and aware so she didn't become a victim."

"Did either of you *consider* that the site this possible-Josie was on might be somewhere other than Venezuela?" Laney demanded. "For God's sake it happens all the time!"

"Yes, of course. But it was the logical starting point in Sylvia's mind. That *is* where Josie was supposed to be going when she disappeared."

Laney actually growled and Griff dropped his head into his hands, elbows on the table. When he looked up his eyes were as serious and somber as she'd ever seen them.

"Dr. Perez, let's get back to my jurisdiction and the local issue. Both Sylvia and Josie were found here in Shutter Lake. Who did Sylvia suspect was responsible for Josie's disappearance?"

There was no reason to hold back, not now that the recording devices were off. It seemed more and more likely that she'd have to run to survive this. She would give them everything she knew before she took off.

"Well, the Windermeres were at the top of her list," Ana admitted. "They've hosted most of the exchange students through the years. It's the most direct connection."

"You leave Mr. and Mrs. Windermere alone," Laney snapped.

Startled, Ana held up her hands in surrender. "Sylvia was using her unique access to find the local connection," she continued. "If not the Windermeres, who else had been close enough to Josie to snatch her?"

"Unique access?" Laney echoed. "As in snooping through the homes of her clients?"

Before Ana could answer, Griff asked, "Were you assisting her in any other manner?"

"My only contribution was to listen as Sylvia sorted theory from fact and to find what I could on the trafficking side."

Laney fumed.

Griff arched an eyebrow. "Go on."

"A few of the trafficked victims I treated were brave enough to give me names." She reached into her purse. "I passed the information on to the authorities at the time."

"But you kept the list anyway?" Laney tilted her head.

She shrugged. "I kept it in my files. It was a natural instinct." Wedged between the names of three operators in California and Texas, Sergio Rojas was listed along with the last known cell phone number she had for her father. "This is all the documentation I have."

Laney plucked up the small plastic bag with the short list of names and numbers. "This is it?"

"I'm sorry. Yes." Ana struggled to maintain eye contact as the helplessness swamped her. There had to be a way to help Laney find Sylvia's killer. "So far, I haven't found a connection between the names on that list and residents of Shutter Lake."

"You realize this could implicate *you* as the connection."

Ana gaped at her friend. Would Laney ever see her the same way again?

"Easy, Holt," Griff said. "You worked on this, even after Sylvia died?" he queried.

"I have," Ana admitted. "I believed Josie was still in trouble and I desperately wanted to find something actionable to bring to you." She shook her head. "I had no idea Josie was already…dead."

Laney tipped her head back and stared at the ceiling a long moment. "You weren't obstructing," she said. "But together we might have gotten to the bottom of this before the killer took aim at Sylvia."

Ana didn't argue. They'd never know. She wanted to hang on to the rest, but she couldn't do that to her friend again. "There's one more thing."

Laney arched her eyebrows and spread her arms wide. "We're still listening."

"Sylvia told me she planned to notify the FBI and she promised to store all her research on a, *umm*, a dead man's switch," she said, recalling the term Troy had used. "Either it didn't work or it hasn't come through yet."

Laney and Griff exchanged a look. "Do you know the name of the FBI agent she spoke with?" Griff asked.

Ana shook her head. "No." She waited as another long look passed between Griff and Laney.

"On it." Laney slapped her hands to the table as she stood. "I'll go back through Sylvia's phone and computer. At the office too." She got up and stalked out of the room.

Griff pinned Ana with another hard gaze as she started to rise. "You stay." She resumed her seat, wondering if he'd changed his mind about charging her. "You hurt her feelings." He leaned his shoulders against the closed door. "I know that's a surprise since she pretends she doesn't have them anymore."

"If I could change the past, I would," she said with complete honesty.

Griff tilted his head. "You're too compassionate to cause pain intentionally." He stepped forward, grabbed the chair and swiveled it around. He sat, straddling the seat, bracing his forearms on the back. "What aren't you telling me?"

"I don't know what you mean."

He sighed. "You're valuable, Ana. I'll tell you this investigation has pulled back the veil on several residents. So far, Laney and I are doing what we can to minimize any long-term damage and keep the community spirit and faith strong."

"That's admirable, Griff. Shutter Lake is better because you're here as the police chief."

He stared at her a long time. She didn't flinch this time, a lifetime of practice serving to keep her emotions, darkest desires and secrets well hidden.

He blinked first. "The city council vetted you and invited you to be a vital leader here. If there's something I need to know to keep you safe, now's the time to share it."

She shook her head. Even if she had the courage to tell him, knowing her secrets would make *him* vulnerable. "Did you find any helpful evidence at my house?"

"Three bullets, just as you heard. Your glass door is repaired. I stuck around for that. We have the bullet that ended up in your fireplace and the one from the railing."

"Do you think you'll get anything on the ballistics?"

"I sent it to the county lab. Time will tell." He stacked his hands. "Did Sylvia suspect anyone other than the Windermeres?"

"Not that I was aware of."

"I hope that's an honest answer, Ana, because someone—maybe someone right here in this town—is targeting you. Literally. It would be easier to protect you if I could narrow the suspect pool."

Ana understood how it might look that way to him. She still hadn't ruled out the possibility that her father had found her and was finally exacting his vengeance. "Griff, I've reviewed my patient files, looking back at appointments and treatments in search of a clue about a local suspect. I don't like the idea that I've been treating a killer."

She'd surprised him with that admission. "Well, I guess we'll all keep digging." he stood, turned the chair around and tucked it under the table. "I've made arrangements to have someone keep an eye on you. Protection," he clarified.

"Thank you." She appreciated the warning.

If Griff had her house under surveillance she would adjust her escape accordingly. This time, when she ran, she could not afford to leave any kind of trail.

CHAPTER ELEVEN

Yolanda came out of a dreamless sleep and rolled over to check the clock. It was just past three a.m., the world quiet and dark and still. Too quiet. Normally Zion would be snoring beside her. His absence must have woken her.

She curled into the pillow, ridiculously relieved that she'd slept for three straight hours. A new record thanks to the medicine Dr. Perez had prescribed. She stretched out and found Zion's pillow cool. He must have been up for some time. She really needed to convince him to set an appointment at the clinic. It couldn't be healthy to bury his grief in work, keeping the same hours he'd kept in his thirties.

No, they weren't old, just older. And grieving. The combination was dreadful.

She heard Zion's voice downstairs, low and intense. Angry. For a moment she thought it was an effect of the medicine. Who would he be speaking to at this hour?

She slipped out of bed and shrugged into her silk robe, determined to bring him back to bed. Staying up all night would only exacerbate the stress of the service and reception this afternoon.

At the top of the stairs she hesitated. His tone had changed again. This wasn't a typical chat with a new client or broker overseas. He was snapping out orders now, in that ruthless tone that tolerated no argument or excuse. And he was giving those orders in French.

She started back to bed when she heard several familiar words. Someone or some deal was dead. Fresh cattle would come in by the weekend for an auction.

What on earth?

As his loyal and devoted wife she sympathized with his need to work through the sharpest edges of their grief. He'd done everything to comfort her, shelter her, while holding the police department and investigators accountable for finding Sylvia's killer.

He made decisions and followed through, she thought, listening to his unyielding voice. His voice turned so cold, she shivered, shrinking back to the bedroom. This side of him had always unnerved her. Whoever was on the other end of that call should realize by now that any argument was futile.

Sylvia and Zion used to argue happily for hours over silly things, debating topics and issues from various points of view. He'd taught her to think for herself and when she made a decision to know why so she could defend her point of view.

It made for loud dinner table discussion once in a while when they found things they would never agree on, but the goal had always been to empower their daughter and make her strong.

They'd done that. Her daughter had been remarkably self-sufficient. She'd become a light within the community, a respected business leader and a champion of those less fortunate.

In the darkness, Yolanda nestled into the chair near the window, tucking her feet up under the robe. What on earth had come between Zion and Sylvia in those last few weeks? She'd asked him about it over a dinner of homemade pizza and he'd flicked it away, as if Sylvia's temper didn't matter to him at all.

She knew that wasn't true. From the day she was born, he'd always been respectful and mindful of Sylvia's feelings.

Yolanda walked into the house cradling Sylvia's dog in the crook of her arm. The little guy looked so healthy and happy, yet he only had a few weeks to live.

A tear slid down her cheek and she quickly swiped it away. Better if Sylvia didn't find her crying when she came home from school. Yolanda set the dog on the floor and unclipped the leash. He trotted to his water bowl and then curled up in his bed to wait for his little girl.

Oh her heart was already breaking.

"What did the vet say?" Zion asked as he crouched to scratch the dog's ears.

"Bone cancer. A few weeks at best." She sniffled. "Sylvie will be devastated."

"No chance of treatment?"

She shook her head. "Well, his lungs were clear today on the x-ray. If we amputate, we might get another few months, but there's no guarantee and the recovery would be stressful for him. It seems like a lot to ask of such a little guy."

"It does." He scooped up the dog, cradling him gently in his arms.

"Sylvie will be so upset," Yolanda said. "Maybe we should get a second opinion."

"There's no need to drag it out. Bone cancer only means suffering. For him and all of us too." He tickled the dog's belly. "I'll handle it. You know I'd do anything to spare you and Sylvie." He shifted the little dog around and snapped his neck.

"Zion!"

"Quick and painless," he said. "Better for everyone." He strode out to the back yard and laid the limp body of the dog on the grass under a shade tree. "I'll bury him now and we'll tell her he ran away."

"How is that any better?"

"Quick and painless," he repeated. "Better than letting our little girl watch him die slowly. She has other, healthy animals here to distract her."

"You didn't give her any chance to say goodbye."

"Yolanda," he snapped out her name like a whip. "Enough. It's done. Watching him waste away would have been worse for all of us."

Yolanda hugged her knees to her chest. She hadn't thought of that day in ages, had deliberately blocked it from her mind. Sylvia had been so sad when her dog never came home. She'd made posters and as a family they'd searched for hours and hours over the following days.

Yolanda rubbed at the ache in her chest as she recalled her

daughter's pain. The dog's fate remained a secret between her and Zion.

She supposed it was natural to think back to that terrible day now, as they prepared to bury their only child. Much like Sylvia had no idea what had happened to her dog, Yolanda had no comprehension of who wanted her daughter dead.

Zion walked in and the bedside lamp caught his features in a slash of light and shadows. His eyes were as cold as his voice had been until he found her sitting in the chair. Instantly, his gaze softened, though a distinct wariness remained when he knelt beside her.

"I thought you were sleeping."

"Me too." Her voice shook with unshed tears and questions too terrible to contemplate.

"Did I wake you?"

Suddenly, she knew the truth would be the wrong answer. "No. Just shaking off another bad dream. The one where she walks in for dinner…"

That was all she had to say before he shushed her and pulled her close to the hard wall of his chest. His embrace had always soothed her in the past, but now her nerves jangled. His hand smoothed her hair, his long fingers massaging the tension from her neck.

Yolanda shivered under his touch, remembering the dog. Her husband was no saint, but surely he hadn't killed his own daughter.

She eased away from him, her hand over his heart.

"Tell me what you need," he said.

"Answers," she replied. "Barring that, I suppose it will just take time."

"We'll get the answers," he vowed, his gaze earnest. "The reward will bring in the right lead."

"It's so much money, Zion."

"Doesn't matter. You know I'd do anything to spare you, my love. Always have, always will."

She turned away, her gaze drawn like a magnet to the spot under the tree where a little dog had been buried to spare Sylvie pain.

Did he realize what he'd said? She told herself the overwhelming grief was twisting the words around in her mind. The sleeping pills must be blurring past and present, reality and nightmare.

Her heart knew the truth and her trust in him, her faith in him shattered.

CHAPTER TWELVE

Wednesday October 17

Early Wednesday morning Ana zipped up her black sheath dress. With an expert touch learned at an early age, she applied her makeup, covering the minor discolorations and scrapes on her face. The only evidence that remained was the bandage on her hand and she switched that out for a smaller, less obvious covering that was a closer match to her skin tone. She scooped her hair into an elegant French twist and finished the look with her pearl necklace and small pearl stud earrings.

On her way to the kitchen, she passed the shoes she'd polished last night and left near the front door, a somber reminder of her responsibilities today. She would catch up on paperwork at the clinic until noon, and then go say her final farewell to a dear friend.

She brewed a cup of coffee, adding a splash of cream today. Not the greatest breakfast, but it would suffice. Her stomach was still too unsettled for any real food.

Last night, restless after the interview, she'd alternately refreshed her phone and email, hoping some helpful clue would arrive from Sylvia. She remained disappointed on that front.

Preparing for the worst, she'd drafted her resignation letter and filed it away, along with a handwritten apology to Laney. Naturally, she hadn't slept well, her mind sifting through every conversation she and Sylvia had ever had about Josie, the trafficking, and what to do next.

Who in Shutter Lake was capable of murdering two people, possibly three if she added in the still-missing Agent Adler? Who would also want to shoot at her?

She yanked her mind away from those questions. It wasn't her job to figure it out. She'd done her part, turning over the little she knew to the police. Her plate was plenty full with simultaneously juggling her role as the town physician and tiptoeing around the issue of how she became an expert on human trafficking.

The only silver lining she could see was successfully giving Laney what she needed without exposing herself to humiliation and deportation. Troy would be pleased and possibly proud.

Peering through the window near the front door, she saw the police car parked at the end of her drive. Griff, true to his word, keeping her safe. Would he still do that if he knew she was only a legal American citizen thanks to superbly forged documents and honorable behavior?

When her coffee was finished, she slipped into her shoes, gathered her purse and headed in to work. Her cell phone rang just as she pulled into the clinic parking lot. Recognizing the number, she answered at once.

"Dr. Perez. This is Troy Duval."

He sounded agitated. "Did you change your mind? Do you need assistance getting to Sylvia's service?"

"No. I won't be attending in person. I've made arrangements to watch the service on a live feed."

The idea sounded both lonely and brilliant. "They're recording it?"

"At Mrs. Cole's request, I'm told."

A practical idea. The events would likely go by in a blur and she'd want to remember the outpouring of support for her daughter's memory.

Troy cleared his throat. "I'd like you to come by after the service. Can you make the time?"

"If it's urgent I can send someone—"

"No, no. I'd prefer to speak with you," he said. "Unlike so many others, you don't seem cowed by the grizzled old man in the haunted house."

She laughed at the image. Troy might be an intimidating hermit and crotchety at times, but he would never be deemed grizzled.

Only a few patients got away with dictating their treatment protocol and Troy was at the top of the list. "I'll call when I'm on my way."

"Thank you, Dr. Perez."

The morning clinic hours raced by and all too soon it was time for Ana to stow the paperwork and leave for the service. This wasn't her first funeral since settling in Shutter Lake, but it was definitely the most personal. She hadn't attended a funeral of someone younger than her since she'd run away from home.

At the church, Ana parked her car in the last available space on the last row. She'd been the primary care physician for too long to ignore which of her patients would appreciate a shorter walk into the church.

She thought of Troy, watching from home, and envied him. He could react however he pleased while she didn't have that same freedom. Yolanda in particular would need support rather than the emotional meltdown Ana felt brewing.

Entering the church, she leaned on the hard lessons of both her early years and medical school, keeping her reactions buried deep behind a mask of serenity.

Yolanda and Zion were tucked away somewhere with the minister, she was sure. Church elders served as ushers, guiding people to fill the pews. Ana had planned to go straight into the sanctuary and sit quietly with her thoughts and memories. She hesitated when she saw Renata walk in with the other Sparkle employees.

Renata had been working tirelessly to keep the business going for the sake of the clients as well as the employees. Ana wondered if Sylvia had been proactive about the fate of her business or if those instructions were lost along with the dead man's switch.

Clustered together, the women looked a bit weepy around the edges, consoling each other before an usher guided them to their seats in the area reserved for the family. They looked so miserable. It left her wondering if there was something more going on. Why didn't they want to sit with Mr. and Mrs. Cole?

She didn't recall Sylvia mentioning any strife between her parents and her employees. Except for the time when Josie, young and new to the staff, was unsure how to interpret Zion's friendly and familiar manners. The girl had mentioned her discomfort to Renata and the situation had been quickly smoothed over by Sylvia.

And a few weeks later Josie disappeared.

Nolan walked over to the church from the coffee shop at the last possible moment. He didn't want to give anyone an opening to talk with him or wonder why he was there. He didn't intend to stop by the gathering at the Cole house afterward. He only wanted to say goodbye to Sylvia.

Again.

What he wouldn't give to touch her silky hair, her petal soft skin one more time.

He stretched out, spent, loving the feel of Sylvia's long legs tangled with his.

All he could smell was her. Her skin, her sheets, her shampoo. She insisted he shower well before he came over. Though she raved about his excellent coffee, she refused to have the smell in her sheets.

He didn't mind. It gave him a deeper enjoyment of the details that were specifically her.

Her mind had drawn him in at first. She was a savvy businesswoman and in a town as set and tidy as Shutter Lake her insistence on discretion was logical.

He would have done whatever she wanted just to spend time with her, in or out of bed. And the complete privacy suited him. He'd been in no hurry to deal with community opinion on their relationship.

He drew circles on her shoulder, her hair a ripple of delicate sensation over his arm. She was thinking, her body relaxed, but her mind had started working again.

"What's on your mind?"

She propped up on her elbow and leaned in, pressing her lips to his. She indulged both of them with a deep, sensual kiss that set his heart racing. He was ready for an encore, slid his hands down her supple body, but she slipped from the bed on a husky laugh.

"I have some work to do." She dragged sexy lavender panties up her lean legs and then shimmied into a pink nightshirt. The Sparkle logo caught the soft light from the bedside lamp. She finger combed her hair, her gaze hungry as she watched him lounging on her bed. "I'm serious," she said, tugging the hem of the long shirt down over her hips. "Get moving. But come back tomorrow."

"I'll see you for coffee in the morning?"

"Of course." She sauntered closer, walked her hands up his chest and around the back of his neck. "I have a dozen cupcakes in my fridge. I can't share those with the girls without coffees."

"I'll have the order ready."

She kissed him. "You really are the best, Nolan."

It was as close as she'd come to declaring feelings. She certainly made him feel unstoppable.

She walked him to the front door and he left, his body still humming and her scent all over him. That heady sensation carried him all the way home before he realized he'd left his cell phone at her place and had to turn around.

Nearing her house, he saw the lights on in her front room.

She was deliberate about keeping business and personal life separate, so he returned to the space just off the road where he normally parked and walked back.

Close to the house, he could hear voices. Odd, since he didn't see a car. Respectful of her strict boundaries, he went around back.

He'd go in through the bedroom window and be back out again before she or her guest noticed.

Grabbing his cell phone, he started to leave when he heard her shouting. The deeper voice of a man rumbled in contrast to hers, but Nolan couldn't pick out the words.

Smooth and cultured, the fury still came through loud and clear.

What the hell?

He heard a slap followed by Sylvia swearing. The man kept talking in those carefully modulated tones. He sounded so reasonable, yet Sylvia remained quiet.

A minute later, Nolan heard a thud. A sniffle. And silence.

Too much silence.

Sylvia was a spitfire. If someone had come to her house and argued with her, she'd still be fuming.

Knowing he shouldn't do it, that she'd likely break up with him as soon as she discovered he was here, he peered around the corner to check on her.

She was on the floor, her nightshirt riding up high on her thighs, a sliver of those lavender panties visible. Her eyes stared sightlessly at the ceiling fan overhead and her hair fanned out as if someone had stroked it into place.

She looked… dead. Her chest didn't rise and fall, no matter that he watched and waited for the movement.

No! The word echoed in his mind as he wept.

He reached for her, desperate to hold her, to shake life back into her. He stopped when he saw the marks on the slim column of her throat.

It was clearly too late.

He touched the silk of her hair, gently pressed his lips to hers in a loving farewell. The reality, the horror, crashed over him. She was gone.

He clapped a hand over his mouth before he started screaming. He had to get out of here. Protect her reputation. Their secret. Aching with the battle to leave when he wanted to stay and look after her, he took his phone and climbed out her bedroom window.

Then he ran, blind with grief.

Someone nudged his shoulder and he got to his feet with the rest of the congregation to sing the next hymn.

Although Dr. Perez had urged him to go to the police, he didn't see how he could help. It wasn't as if he'd seen anything but Sylvia's lifeless body. He'd nearly called in a tip that the kid who'd first confessed to the crime couldn't be the killer when the kid was cleared by other means.

Thankfully.

Sylvia might be dead, but he refused to violate her trust even now. Deputy Chief Holt could eye him with suspicion every time their paths crossed. She knew from the DNA he'd left on Sylvia's sheets that he'd been in the house that night. That would have to be enough for her.

And he'd been *trying* to recall any helpful detail about that voice. It had been deep, authoritative, and otherwise indistinguishable. He'd been listening closely to every customer since, hoping for a flicker of recognition. Even if he told Holt about the mumbling he'd heard, it wouldn't point them to the right person and he'd only implicate himself.

His business would take a hit if people thought for even a minute he'd killed Sylvia. As an entrepreneur, she would scold him for even thinking about taking that kind of chance with his livelihood. From the start, she'd been eager to make suggestions he could use to innovate and improve the bottom line at The Grind. Now she'd never see her ideas come to fruition.

After nearly two weeks, it seemed so ridiculously impossible that she was gone. Yet here he was, singing "Amazing Grace" with the vast majority of Shutter Lake's residents.

When the service finally ended, everyone shuffled out of the church, leaving her parents to stand beside the open casket, quietly weeping.

What if he'd gone out there, to hell with her rules? Would she be alive now, or would they both be dead?

Why the hell had he run? He should have confronted the bastard.

But he'd run.

The investigation remained open, but he couldn't see how it mattered. Finding her killer wouldn't bring her back, wouldn't heal his broken spirit.

Feeling crowded by his thoughts as much as the people moving too slowly toward the doors, Nolan moved away from the general flow of traffic and out a side door.

CHAPTER THIRTEEN

Ana's hand trembled as she knocked on Troy's door. Her emotions were in turmoil after the service. It had been a lovely celebration of Sylvia's life and the minister delivered an inspiring sermon and moving eulogy. None of it changed the fact that Sylvia was gone.

She didn't think Yolanda had heard a word. Ana had grown concerned for her patient as she resisted all attempts at comfort. She hadn't even leaned into Zion the way she'd done through every press conference and prior outing.

Brittle. That was the best word for it. Hopefully the reception wouldn't be too much for her to bear this afternoon.

Troy called out for Ana to come in and when she closed the door behind her, he asked her to throw the deadbolt. "Thanks for coming so quickly," he said, urging her to join him in the great room.

"Are you hurting?" she asked, concerned now.

"No more than usual," he replied. "I put tea on when the service ended."

"Thank you."

So the live feed from the church must have worked. Ana had

never seen him so animated. He was always rather deliberate and careful with his words and movement, as if he might draw the wrong kind of attention.

He impatiently waited for her to sit down and take the cup of tea. What was bothering him? She'd blame it on the service, but he'd called her hours beforehand. Had he thought of something pertinent to Sylvia's investigation? If so, she'd have to call Laney immediately.

"Forgive me. I'm rattled," he admitted. "I feel particular sympathy for Yolanda and Zion. Outliving a child is the worst form of heartache."

Ana would take his word on that. She'd decided never to have children of her own. The world was cold and harsh and she'd never had the full confidence that the goodness she added would be enough to offset the evil perpetrated by her father and his associates.

Troy ignored his cup of tea and lowered his voice. "I found Sylvia's dead man switch."

Ana froze. "She stashed it here."

"Yes." Troy's eyes gleamed with excitement. "She was so, so clever."

It made perfect sense. In addition to his state-of-the-art security system, Troy was always home. His reputation as a grumpy recluse only added another layer of protection to the information.

"Have you looked at it?"

"No." He shook his head. "Didn't seem right. Sylvia's business was her own."

Except when it involved the world Ana had escaped. "How?"

"I found a flash drive as well as an envelope addressed to you."

"Me?" Ana carefully placed her tea cup on the tray and reluctantly accepted the notecard Troy handed over. Sylvia had used Sparkle stationery and Ana's name was indeed written in script on the envelope.

"Sylvia's handwriting," she murmured, tracing the three letters. An odd fear filled her as she turned the envelope over. "I'll open it later." It seemed like something that should be done in absolute privacy. "Where is the flash drive?"

Troy reached into the breast pocket of his shirt and withdrew a flash drive in the shape of a unicorn head with a sparkling rainbow horn.

She tugged off the character's horn and exposed the USB tab. Leave it to Sylvia.

What had her friend stashed here? And where would it lead the investigation? "I'll take this straight to the police," she promised.

"What? No, you can't do that."

"It's the right thing to do." She wouldn't give Laney any cause to doubt her again. At least until she disappeared.

"It's not. You can't," Troy sputtered. "You can't hand it over until you know what's there."

She gave him a long, assessing look. "You *have* opened this."

He dropped his gaze to the fire. "Only to make sure there was in fact something on it."

"What did you find?"

"Several folders organized by numbers. Nothing like her numbering system for clients," he added. "The numerical system didn't jive with the pattern she uses for my invoice anyway."

Interesting. "I'm sure the police will figure it out."

"Be smart about this, Dr. Perez. If you leave here and go to the police station, you run the risk that the killer will find out and suspect something."

A chill raised the hair at the back of her neck. Griff believed she'd been shot at for doing just that on Monday even though she'd made previous house calls for Troy. Would the police officer tailing her be any real deterrent to a killer determined to snip loose ends?

The killer had definitely been familiar to Sylvia. She'd allowed him into her home late at night when she was only in her sleep shirt. "Did you save the files to your hard drive?"

"No. But we can do that if that makes you feel better."

"It might." Ana toyed with the little unicorn. She wanted to take a peek at the information, to verify there wasn't anything that would implicate her dubious citizenship. It was highly unlikely that Sylvia had figured out the whole truth or even cared about Ana's past.

Thinking about the fit Laney would have if *she* figured it out and the cold bite of handcuffs on her wrists, Ana decided not to chance it. "I can get the information to the police without going by the station."

"If you intend to pop it in the mail, I could do that myself."

"I'm not about to take that risk." Or waste the day or two it would take. "But I would like to back up the information to a secure cloud service if you'll allow me to use your computer."

"Of course."

He insisted on walking with her to his office. She sat down in the executive chair behind the desk, admiring the rich caress of the leather upholstery. This space suited him with the view of the mountains through the wall of windows on the opposite wall.

As Troy had said, the folders were numbered. At first glance each folder contained a series of photos. Once Ana had saved the data with a patient name and identification number she ejected the flash drive. "Hopefully the police will understand what Sylvia stored here right away."

"If you send that intel through cloud access they'll know you were involved," Troy pointed out.

Looking up, she met his gaze. "That's my last resort, and I'll use it only if the drive is lost or compromised. I can get this drive directly into police custody without being caught."

"You seem confident." His gaze narrowed. "What are you planning?"

Suddenly she was confident. Getting Sylvia's notes to the police gave her hope that her killer would be locked up and this mess would soon be behind them.

"Skepticism becomes you," she teased, tapping her brow where his furrowed. "Quite scholarly. Believe me, I don't want to be forced out of my position here anymore than I want you to be drawn into this mess."

He folded his arms, unconvinced.

Standing, she changed the subject. "Would you like to ride with me to the reception at the Cole's? We don't have to stay long."

"No, thank you. Yolanda's grief during the service was too much. I would be no comfort to her."

She tucked the letter and flash drive into her purse and Troy walked her to the door. Opening it, she paused, allowing a blast of refreshing autumn air into his home. "Thank you, so very much."

He frowned again, his gaze aimed toward the police cruiser parked on the road outside his gate. "I've done little to earn any gratitude."

"On the contrary," she said. "You could have thrown this away."

"And let a murderer skate?" His expression soured. "That's appalling."

She agreed. "You gave Sylvia guidance and friendship." Though he shook his head, his gaze full of regret, she plowed on. "You were important to her, a bright spot rather than a routine. And I'm thankful for your advice to take care of who I am now so the past can't drag me back down."

"Stay careful," he said.

"The next time I see you, I'll bring something sweet," she said. Better to exude confidence than to leave him with more worries.

Alone in her car, she gave in to the quiver of trepidation and clutched the steering wheel to steady her hands. Knowing Sylvia as she did, she wasn't concerned with the information on the unicorn. She was far more worried about the letter and the information Sylvia didn't trust to electronics and digital databases.

Ana only made it as far as the gates at the end of Troy's long driveway before she pulled over to read the letter from Sylvia. She shouldn't open it, not when she was still so raw from the service and had to attend a reception. She opened it anyway.

Dear Ana,

It's October 2nd. If you're reading this, I lost the battle. Forgive me for not opening up and sharing these details sooner, but now it's time for you to make sure we win the war. For Josie and all the others.

It isn't easy discovering that my lifelong hero is actually the lowest form of scum. At this point, I'm positive the local connection to the trafficking ring is my father. No, I haven't been sniffing cleaning solvents, I haven't hit my head and I'm not delusional.

A couple weeks ago, I overheard him mention Josie's school in Venezuela during a phone call. He tried to blow it off, claiming he intended to donate money for renovations or something. I didn't buy it, not after checking the video at the office. I can't believe the way he leered at her the first couple times he brought over lunch after I hired her.

I gave him hell that day, called him names and eventually fished out enough details to be sure he'd done it. My persistence sent him over the edge. He was furious and went on a rant. He said 'someone like Josie' could be taken because she wouldn't be missed and her disappearance would never matter. He said I needed to grow up and take the blinders off. Girls like her would always be replaceable.

Ana blinked away tears. Zion sounded so much like her father.

He swore I'll never find any proof of his involvement. And I haven't. He told me to forget Josie, that I'll never see her again. I went out to the house the other day and sat on the deck, visiting with Mom. All I could think was that he could be right. They have nearly one hundred acres and he could have buried her anywhere out there.

I had to leave in a rush before I blurted it all out to Mom. Even if she believed me, what could she do? You have no idea how much I want to make him pay for this.

Yesterday, he cornered me at the office. He knows I've been looking into the other missing teenagers. Maybe he tapped my phone or bugged my office or something. He ordered me to back off 'or else'. We fought again and I dared him to try and stop me. You know I'll never quit until we find her.

No. Sylvia didn't quit anything once she'd set her mind on it.

Dad has always been smart and hardnosed and a little arrogant. I never would have believed it before, but I can see now that some facet of his nature twisted into cruelty somewhere along the way. Maybe it was always there and he just got careless about hiding it. Or maybe I've simply learned to look for it. Either way, he isn't acting like a man getting into trouble for the first time.

Without real evidence, he won't be caught. I'm hustling tonight, in case he does something outrageous to drag my name through the mud or pin Josie's disappearance on me or who knows what. Arrogant and furious aren't a good combination.

Well I'm sure I sound paranoid by now. You know I'm not. I compiled all the articles and all our theories and put them on a flash drive along with everything I could download on Dad. If you only have the letter, someone is holding out on you.

I trust you'll figure it out.

One thing isn't on the drive. I planted a voice-activated recorder pen in Dad's car. There's another one in the mug of pens in his office. I haven't been able to retrieve that one yet. He made two calls from his car in the last week to someone named Sergio Rojas. They talked for a couple of minutes each time about cattle shipments. I'm hoping the name clicks for you after working with trafficking victims.

Ana closed her eyes as the evil face of her father filled her mind. All she could do was breathe through it. Even here, in her final letter, Sylvia was careful to protect her secrets.

I stashed the recording device from his car in your office at the clinic. It's a slim black pen in the back of your center drawer. Maybe the recordings along with the flash drive and this letter will be enough to convince Chief McCabe or the FBI to investigate Dad. Special Agent Adler has my earlier notes, but so far he hasn't gotten back to me.

Whatever happens, protect yourself. Don't let this blow back on you or upset everything you've made of your life.

Don't give Dad that kind of win. One of us has to take him down and survive to help others. If you're reading this, I guess it has to be you.

Your sister in spirit,

Sylvia

Ana's heart pounded in her ears. She read the letter again, her pulse stuttering at the sight of her father's name on the page, written in Sylvia's hand.

Zion Cole, human trafficker?

Sylvia must be mistaken, and yet, she was confident enough to put it in writing.

Ana forced herself to think through Sylvia's allegations logically as she drove to the Cole home for the reception. Zion certainly fit the profile they had of the killer. Taller than Sylvia, familiar to her, and though he was sixty, he remained fit and strong.

Edgy, Ana walked into the Cole home. A member of the mortuary team was stationed at the door, with a guest book. She signed in, pleased her hand didn't shake.

The somber mood of the guests and the carefully modulated voices soothed her, slowing her racing thoughts. Aromas of both savory and sweet comfort foods floated on the air, expertly catered by the team from San Francisco. Ana's stomach cramped with nerves over what she was about to attempt.

Could Laney still use the recorded information if Ana brought the device out of the house? She probably should have called Laney first. But Sylvia had put this on her. Only Ana, having grown up in the heart of those horrors, really understood the misery victims suffered.

She didn't care about protecting herself, her career, or her reputation anymore. She would happily sacrifice all of that to know her father and his cronies were in fact, done. Out of business forever.

This had grown beyond finding justice for Sylvia. This was about justice for all the girls she knew hadn't made it out of those chains alive. All those girls, nameless and forgotten, deserved more. Here was her opportunity to make a difference. At last.

Scanning the expansive great room, it seemed nearly everyone who'd been to the funeral was milling about, along with many others. She imagined the entire community would come and go before the end of the day.

Ana spotted Yolanda standing between the kitchen and dining room, visiting with the mayor, his new assistant Gracie, and Dana. Yolanda's eyes were puffy and her cheeks pale, though she tried to smile as they conversed. Ana hoped Dana could convince the woman to sit down.

Then her eyes lit on Zion, outside on the deck, surrounded by several familiar faces. She had to hold back a scream of rage as memories of her father in similar situations fogged over the reality.

She wasn't a child any longer. She was an educated adult, armed with knowledge and strength, and backed up by a functional justice system.

She focused on her intention and made a to-do list in her head. First, take the voice recorder pen from Zion's office. Second, stop by the clinic for the pen Sylvia had stashed there. Third, go directly to the police station. After that, not much else mattered today.

Flanked by Mayor Jessup and Dana, Yolanda walked toward a seating area in front of the fireplace. To Ana's eye, she seemed a fraction more at ease than she'd been during the service. Maybe it was the white wine in her hand, or more likely, the stories guests were sharing about her daughter.

For the first time in years, Ana wondered if her mother had ever grieved for her. Likely she'd been denied the opportunity and space. There was no telling what lies her father would have given to cover up her escape.

She chatted quietly with other guests as she alternately studied Zion and the closed door of his home office. Sylvia believed their fathers had cruel business and brutality in common. Ana wondered if she ever would have seen that side of him.

Her father had been the raw end of the equation. Gathering up girls, testing them and often breaking them before moving them along to buyers. She'd known Zion for years and never once sensed he was the refined, cultured end of that violent industry. She'd cared for the man through annual physicals, a bout of flu and a knee injury. She'd shared meals and jokes with him at fundraisers and other community events. And she'd administered vaccination boosters before he'd traveled out of the country.

Bile burned in the back of her throat, thinking she might have assisted him in some small way when he was going out shopping for girls as casually as other people shopped for cars.

If Sylvia was right, he'd fooled everyone, even his wife. The idea of a man as admired as Zion Cole coordinating with Rojas for the purpose of selling girls like cattle was reprehensible.

Today would be the beginning of his downfall. Her only regret would be piling more grief onto Yolanda.

Laney was making her way out and Ana was tempted to hand her the flash drive. She could do it in a way that no one would notice. No one but a person who might just have been manipulating everyone from the start.

Zion, occupied with the service, the private interment, and his struggling wife had no way of knowing where Ana had spent the last hour. She might feel reassured by that if her father hadn't had her tailed time and again before she'd finally escaped.

She'd learned at an early age that men in power had access. And men in powerful criminal organizations had eyes everywhere.

Those men also had an obligation to keep up the legitimate façade. She wouldn't have another opportunity like this, with Zion distracted by a house full of people. This was her best chance of grabbing an advantage that would turn the tide of the war, as Sylvia put it. Easing her way across the great room toward the office, she stopped frequently to visit with other guests, wondering how they'd react if she blurted out the news that they were standing in the home of a criminal.

Nearing the closed doors of the office, she waited for an opening to slip inside. She'd decided it would be best to fake a call from the clinic. Pulling her phone from her purse, she peered at the screen. No one was close enough to know her phone hadn't made a sound.

She turned the door handle and found it locked. Angry and hurt, her first thought was the locked door signified an admission of guilt, though it was hardly evidence. Logically, it made sense for any normal businessman to want to keep his workspace off limits when his home was full of people coming and going.

Momentarily stumped, Ana picked up a glass of sparkling water and joined the group of people closest to Yolanda waiting to express their sympathy and support.

She briefly considered searching other parts of the house, just in case she found some other type of evidence. Sylvia had given Josie a silver poodle pin as an encouragement of sorts. Maybe Zion had kept it as a memento. He wouldn't be the first killer to do something like that.

Snooping through the house was a far cry from slipping into an office to take a call from the clinic. How was she going to get in there? Even if she knew how to pick a lock, she didn't see how she'd manage the feat without drawing attention. She was stuck hoping that what Sylvia had collected so far would be enough for Laney to get a search warrant for Zion's office.

After speaking briefly with Yolanda and encouraging her to rest, she turned for the door, only to be stopped by Zion. Her blood ran cold, then hot and she struggled to stay in control.

He was a handsome man. Tall and lean, his short silver hair gleamed against the sun-warmed skin of a man who enjoyed the outdoors. For hiking or burying bodies, she wondered. He bore no resemblance to her rough-talking, craggy-faced father whose beady eyes revealed the snake under his skin.

She let him draw her out through the doors that opened onto the deck and down the steps into the backyard. They stopped under the shade of a tree near the fence. Sylvia's comment from the letter that Josie could be buried out here echoed through her mind.

"I'm worried for Yolanda," he said. "She isn't sleeping and I think it's affecting her thought processes."

"In what way?"

He flung an arm toward the house. "This reception is a prime example. It's only making things worse."

"I disagree." Ana continued as he glared down his straight nose at her. "The reception was smart. It allows the two of you to grieve with the community. It gives you both closure. Tomorrow, we'll all start to move on."

"Possibly," he muttered. "The lack of sleep is definitely affecting her health."

Ana knew Yolanda had signed the documents allowing her to share medical information with her husband, but after reading Sylvia's letter, she would tread carefully. "I changed her prescription. This is an unthinkable tragedy for both of you. Time is the only real healer in this situation."

"Time and justice." His pale blue gaze darkened, skating over the guests closer to the house. "Someone must know something."

Ana's heart pounded. "You should speak with Chief McCabe about that." She sipped the sparkling water to keep from blurting out something that might reveal her true thoughts. According to his daughter, Zion was an expert at hiding his true nature. If she made a mistake, he would pounce. "Honestly, I'm concerned for both of you," she said. "Have you been sleeping?"

"Better than her," Zion admitted. "I'm her husband. Since our wedding day, it's been my job to provide and care and comfort. I want to fix it."

"This day will forever be one of the worst of her life," she murmured, catching sight of Yolanda just inside the doors that separated the house and deck. "Yours too. I'm afraid the nature of death is that it is unfixable."

He glared at her and then shook his head, his shoulders rounding as if the weight of the world had finally become too much. "I should never have agreed to this. That crowd of people can't possibly be helping. She's only wallowing, denying the inevitable."

"On the contrary," Ana replied. "Knowing your daughter was well-loved, admired and respected should bring both of you a great deal of comfort."

"I guess I'll defer to your expertise." He turned that intense gaze on her directly. "If you see any signs of emotional breakdown, you'll tell me?"

Emotional breakdown? Ana had to work hard to hold her nerve. Was the man laying groundwork for incompetence in case Sylvia's accusations surfaced and Yolanda saw through him? "May I ask why you're so concerned? It must be more than the decision to have people over."

He pulled off the expression of a devoted husband perfectly. "It all goes back to the sleeplessness, I suppose. She's been pulling away, distant. She was distraught and confused in the middle of the night and again this morning. It's not like her."

"That sounds as if she was caught in a twilight," Ana said. "It's more of a physical side-effect than an emotional concern. Considering the medication adjustment, it's no surprise. Things will settle out."

From her purse, she heard the chime of her cell phone. "If you'll excuse me."

He tipped his head as she walked away from him and up the steps to the deck. Recognizing Laney's number, she answered right away. "This is Dr. Perez."

"Ana, Laney. Where are you?"

"I'm at the Cole house."

Laney cursed. "I need you to come by the station. And bring your phone."

Ana didn't dare reply or ask questions. Not out here where she could be overheard by Zion or anyone else he might have in his pocket. "I'm on my way."

CHAPTER FOURTEEN

Yolanda's eyes burned. She didn't feel as if she had any tears left to shed. She was grieving for more than her daughter today. She could not shed the horrific likelihood that her husband killed Sylvia in some twisted notion of protection.

It didn't make sense. She had no proof, no motive. And yet she suddenly believed it with all her heart and soul. It was as if Sylvia had whispered in her ear during a moment of fitful sleep. The instinct would not abate. Would not be dismissed.

A small voice in her head tried to convince her she was wrong, but the idea had taken root and branched out, connecting all the trivial and inconsequential details into a strong working theory.

"Someone robbed and murdered my daughter?" That had been his first question when Chief McCabe and Deputy Chief Holt had delivered the terrible news. The moment bounced around in her mind. *"So what you're telling us is that you don't have any evidence. You don't have any idea who did this?"*

They still didn't. All that reward money and not one credible lead. He'd made such a case, insisting that only a private investigator could get to the truth. Dear God, who did he intend to set up to take the blame for his crime?

No one had ever questioned her or Zion as potential suspects. A perk of being original Shutter Lake founders, she supposed. She thought he'd been home in his office the night Sylvia had died, but he could have come and gone whenever he pleased. They'd designed the house with an exterior door so he could conduct business and interact with his clients without having to traipse through the family space.

The entire town was traipsing through their home now.

She watched as everyone spoke with him, expressing sympathy and hope for Sylvia's killer to come to justice. He remained too confident even as he griped about the lack of progress on the case. She'd been too grief-stricken to see the imbalance.

And what on earth had he been saying to Dr. Perez a few minutes ago outside in the yard? She had to know, had to find a way to share her concerns before Zion did something else.

As the doctor passed by, Yolanda stepped into her path. "Thank you so much for being here." She clasped the doctor's hands. "It means..." She let her voice trail off, let herself sway to the side.

"Yolanda, you should sit down." Dr. Perez guided her to a seat closer to the sunshine pouring in through the wall of windows separating the house from the deck. "I understand how important this gathering is, but you shouldn't overdo."

"But I slept last night," she said quietly. "Three hours straight."

Dr. Perez arched an eyebrow. Not a big movement, but Yolanda was watching for any sign. "Zion told you differently?"

"He was only concerned that you were restless and awake during the night. Your sleeplessness must have coincided."

Not a chance. Dread danced along her spine. It could be nothing, or it could be the first sign of more trouble.

Dr. Perez pressed a cool hand to her forehead. "I assured him it was simply the medication. Both of you need time and care to heal. I'm sure after this, you'll sleep soundly tonight."

"Out of sheer exhaustion," Yolanda said.

"It becomes a factor, yes," Dr. Perez agreed.

"That should come as a relief." Yolanda dabbed at her eyes as hot, angry tears spilled over her lashes. She knew what she had to do. There was only one place she could safely give voice to her worst fears.

And in sharing her theory of a crime, Dr. Perez would have to notify the police.

Glancing around, she saw Zion outside. Now was her best chance of success. "I'll be fine, doctor." Standing quickly, she feigned weakness and pitched toward Ana. The doctor caught her.

"Yolanda." Immediately, Dr. Perez shifted into an assessment. "Yolanda, what is it?"

The people closest to them turned, concern and sympathy stamped on every face. "I feel faint. My vision…" She waved a hand in front of her face. "My goodness. I can't see so well."

"Sit down a moment." Dr. Perez eased her back into the chair, crouching in front of her. She asked a guest for a cool cloth. "We'll take a minute and see if the symptom passes."

"A-all right." She needed the doctor to get her out of this house.

Dr. Perez took her pulse. "Do you have a blood pressure monitor on hand?"

"No," Yolanda replied. Someone pressed the damp, cool cloth to the back of her neck. "You know Zion and I are in perfect health. Take me to the clinic," she murmured so only the doctor could hear.

Dr. Perez pursed her lips, meeting her gaze. "Your heart is racing, Yolanda. I'm sure you're simply overtired, but I'd feel better if you let me take a closer look at the clinic."

"Oh, but all our guests…"

"They only want to see you well." Dr. Perez helped her to her feet. "Lean on me now. Your husband can handle things here."

Yolanda wondered if she'd imagined the hard edge in the doctor's voice as they moved toward the front door. So far, Zion hadn't noticed the commotion.

Once in the doctor's car, Yolanda kept checking the side mirror as they drove away from the house, more than half-afraid she'd see Zion racing after them.

"Are you comfortable?" Dr. Perez queried.

Yolanda nodded. It was all she could do to keep her mouth shut until they were in the exam room at the clinic. A young nurse took her blood pressure and pulse again and Dr. Perez listened to her heart. When they were alone, the door shut, and presumably her medical chart on the tablet the doctor held, she made sure she could speak freely.

"Anything I say in here is confidential, right?"

"In regards to your medical record, yes," Dr. Perez replied. "If you were to confess to a crime or threaten to hurt yourself I would be obligated to pass that along to the authorities or take appropriate action."

"Good." Yolanda steeled herself for the reaction to what she was about to say. "Zion killed Sylvia. I'm sure of it."

Dr. Perez gaped at her. "Mrs. Cole-"

"It's true." She grabbed a tissue, just in case. This wasn't the time for tears or hysterics. She needed her voice to be clear and strong. "Dr. Perez, you must believe me. I can't prove it. Yet." She hopped down from the exam table and paced the small room. "There must be something in his office or at her house that will link him to the crime. He staged it to look like a robbery, but he killed her. I know it in my heart…in my soul. Can you tell Deputy Chief Holt to investigate Zion? You two are friends, right?"

Dr. Perez had closed her mouth, though her deep brown eyes remained round with surprise. "Right. We are."

"I'm not crazy."

"No, Yolanda, you're not crazy."

"Then why aren't you leaping into action? Make the call, I beg you." Yolanda sat down in the chair, putting her at eye level with the doctor. "You don't believe me."

"I'd like to hear why you believe it," Dr. Perez said with her typical, maddening calm that was usually reassuring.

"He's locking his office. Hasn't done that in years. He's been driving more. I heard him on the phone last night talking about cattle of all things. And he told me."

Now Dr. Perez's eyebrows arched. "I beg your pardon?"

She waved her hands in the air as if erasing her chaotic claims. "In order, Yolanda," she coached herself. She laced her fingers, breathing deep. "Sylvia and Zion were in some sort of a fight just before she died. They'd had disagreements through the years but nothing like this. She refused to be around him at all this time."

Yolanda wrung her hands, twisting the tissue she held until it crumbled. When she dared to look at Dr. Perez, she didn't see skepticism or even sympathy in her eyes, but thoughtful consideration.

"Go on," the doctor said simply.

"Well, I was concerned, naturally. Zion kept telling me it was a business issue. They didn't see eye to eye about her plans to expand. When the police asked us that…that day, he said there wasn't any trouble in her business."

"I didn't realize she was planning to expand."

"Neither did I, but I believed him. Sylvia always had big ideas and bigger dreams. Maybe if I hadn't stuck my head in the sand she'd still be alive. Instead, I told myself to stay out of it."

"Why?"

"Because business was their connection, their language. I should have seen this time the trouble was different." Another wave of tears threatened and Yolanda was no match for it this time. Dr. Perez let her sob for several minutes.

"You should tell all of this to the police," Dr. Perez said quietly. "Once they eliminate Zion as a suspect it will put your mind at ease."

Yolanda shook her head. "If he hears about my suspicions, if he learns I spoke with anyone, he'll kill me too."

"Why would he kill you? He seems to adore you so."

"To protect his interests, his reputation, his glorious achievements," she cried. "That's always been everything to him. The rest of it, the money, the house," she spread her arms wide, "even Sylvia and me, is all just window-dressing." She blew out a breath. Standing, she wrapped her arms around her middle. "Dr. Perez, you and Sylvia were close."

"Yes."

"Did she ever mention the dog that ran away when she was young?"

"Yes, actually. When I thought about getting a dog, she recommended a cat because they're happier inside the house and the shedding would keep her in business."

Yolanda chuckled. "That sounds like my girl." She met the doctor's kind gaze. The compassion in those dark brown eyes gave her courage. "That dog didn't run away. Zion killed it." She swallowed. "With his bare hands. In front of me. Then he buried it before Sylvie got home from school. All to spare her the pain of watching the dog suffer and die from cancer."

"That is…"

"Horrific." Yolanda finished for her. "It took me years to get over it. Sylvie was miserable anyway believing her dog had run off and didn't love her." She paused, determined to make her point clear. "He said something in that moment after he'd strangled that poor dog. He said that he'd do anything to protect us.

"Last night, he said those same words to me when he thought I was up after having another nightmare."

"And you believe his choice of words last night is an admission of guilt?"

"I don't believe he planned to murder our daughter," she confessed with a weary shake of her head. "However, I think it reveals his mindset. I cannot fathom the circumstance that would push him to kill his only child or if that is what he was thinking about last night. I do know he's done something dreadful to protect us from a perceived threat to all we have. I believe killing her was that something."

Dr. Perez tapped her index finger against the edge of the tablet.

"Please say something," Yolanda pleaded as the doctor remained silent.

"Do you fear for your life at home alone with Mr. Cole?"

"Not unless he finds out what I've told you."

"Well, he won't hear it from me."

"It's so hard to think, to believe…" She just couldn't say the words again. "Chief McCabe has implied that Sylvie knew her attacker and she'd let the person into her home. My daughter was too smart to do something like that."

Dr. Perez said, "If you'd like, I can have you placed under observation here. Once you're settled in the room, I can arrange for Laney and the chief to come by and take your statement. No one else will ever know. I can even keep Zion from being alone with you."

Yolanda nodded her agreement with the plan. "Zion won't like it. He'll make things difficult for you."

"I'll handle it. My job is your health."

"All right." She blotted tears from her eyes. What she wouldn't give to stop crying. "Did Sylvia tell you why she was angry with Zion?"

She watched Dr. Perez carefully. The woman was a professional, to be sure. Competent, kind. Warm and serious. And always honest. Yolanda saw the answer before her world imploded.

"Yes."

Yolanda struggled to breathe. "She had a very good reason to be angry with her father, didn't she?"

"Yes."

Her anguished wail filled the room and this time when Yolanda fainted, it wasn't an act.

Ana moved swiftly to get Yolanda situated in one of the private suites before Zion was notified that his wife would be staying the night in the clinic.

She had just finished making arrangements with Laney, using the desk phone in her office, when he barged into the clinic. Where was the armed cop in her hallway now that she needed one?

"Let me see her," Zion demanded, looming over her desk.

"Not yet," Ana replied. "We're still assessing her condition and I've called in a specialist," she improvised.

"She needs *me*," he insisted. "She'll feel better knowing I'm with her."

"I'm sure you're right." Ana marveled that she didn't choke on the words.

Zion could be intimidating when he wanted to be, but her staff knew she was the final authority here. Zion knew it too. Still, he argued his point for several more minutes before she managed to guide him back to an available exam room to wait.

Ana gave him credit. He was either an excellent actor or he was genuinely concerned for his wife. Regardless, she could not discount the allegations piling up against him. She didn't want to.

She didn't have much time to come up with a reasonable medical cause for her decision to isolate Yolanda. While he waited in the exam room, she made a few calls and asked a cardiologist to come give a second opinion. Yolanda's real symptoms and values supported the decision, though she would owe the man a big favor for coming out to the Shutter Lake clinic. Finally, feeling tighter than a bowstring, she invited Zion to her office to discuss the plans for his wife.

She wondered if the voice recorder Sylvia had stowed in her desk had some battery life left. It might help to have documentation of this conversation. Yolanda and Sylvia knew him best and they both considered him capable of heinous, exploitative crimes, including murder. His wife and daughter might not have delivered actionable proof of his crimes, but assuming Zion knew Rojas, Ana wasn't about to tempt fate.

"What is going on here, Dr. Perez?"

"Your wife had an episode earlier today at your home. She was faint and complained of tunnel vision."

"I warned you," Zion snapped. "I stood out there and told you she was in trouble."

"You did."

"I want to take her home. She won't rest here like she will in our bed."

Ana nodded as if his opinion might actually factor into her decision. "If I was sure we were only dealing with exhaustion, I would send her home right now."

"What else could it be?"

"We don't know. That's why she's staying here," Ana replied. "Most likely, if it is exhaustion compounded by grief, fluids and rest will have her up and about in no time. However, her heart was racing and she's complained of vision trouble. It's possible the stressful circumstances have triggered an underlying condition. The specialist is on his way. I'm sure you'll agree it's in Yolanda's best interests to remain with us until we know for sure."

"Yes, of course." To her shock, tears welled in Zion's eyes. "I can't lose her too. She's everything."

The declaration gave Ana little comfort. "Good, good." She stood and came around her desk. "Someone will be with her all night, I promise."

"Me." Zion stood as well.

"I'm sorry, no. That's just not possible. We'll keep you informed of her progress."

"You'll stay with her? Please. Promise me."

"That's my plan. I'll keep you informed and let you know the moment you can see her."

Once Zion was through the front door, Ana turned to the nurse running reception. "Who's next?"

"Exam room three. I've taken care of the vitals."

Ana picked up the tablet and tapped the icon to see the patient information. The name and details popped up on the screen. She wasn't sure if she wanted to laugh or weep as she walked into the room.

CHAPTER FIFTEEN

Laney glanced over her shoulder as the door opened. The relief on Ana's face was nearly comical. She might have laughed if she wasn't still pissed off at her friend for hiding pertinent information on a murder case.

Although, what Ana had eventually given them wasn't proving all that relevant after all.

"Thanks for coming," she said.

"A little early for that," Laney replied. She'd established a makeshift desk on the exam room table and was comparing Ana's cell phone records with the log from Sylvia's phone. "Zion didn't see me come in."

"Good." Ana didn't move, seemingly rooted in place at the center of the room. "Have you found anything helpful?"

"Not so far. There's no action on Sylvia's cell phone after six-thirty the evening of October third. She was found by Renata Fernandez between seven-thirty and eight a.m. on the fourth."

"Time of death was well before Renata found her," Ana said.

"I'm capable of reading a coroner's report," Laney muttered, regretting it immediately. "Sorry. I'm struggling to wrap my head around why Yolanda thinks Zion killed their daughter."

"I'm sure she'll tell you everything. She's convinced he's guilty."

"McCabe is talking with her now." Laney looked up from the screens. "You said there was something else?"

Ana took a step closer, extending an envelope. "Sylvia left this letter for me."

Laney hesitated. Whatever it was, Ana wasn't happy about sharing. "When did you receive it?" If she'd been sitting on this too, Laney might actually charge her with obstruction, to hell with McCabe's sensibilities.

"Today. Just before I went over to the Coles for the reception." She wrapped her arms around her middle as if she'd taken a punch to the gut.

She turned the envelope over. "There's no postmark."

"Just read it," Ana pleaded.

Laney did. Then she read it again. Maybe her friend had been sucker punched, she thought, reading through it a third time. Assuming Sylvia wasn't paranoid or delusional, this letter identified her father as the probable killer. "I'll need to keep this."

"I figured as much."

"She left this with Mr. Duval?"

Ana nodded.

"And the voice-recorder and flash drive?"

"I have both." She reached into her pocket and withdrew a colorful unicorn-shaped flash drive and what appeared to be a normal pen. "I tried to get the voice recorder she planted in Zion's office during the reception, but the door was locked."

"And?" Laney prompted. Her friend didn't have much of a poker face lately.

"And I uploaded the flash drive to a secure cloud, just in case something happened. An account only I can access."

Laney pocketed the devices and looked back at the letter. "What does she mean about blowback?"

"In the past, I've had run-ins with unsavory people who mistreated and enslaved women and girls. People who would kill me if they found me."

"Ana." Laney's frustration and anger drained away at the blend of fear and defiance welling in Ana's eyes. "Why didn't you say something earlier? We can arrange for more protection—"

"No. Despite the mess on Monday night, this is about Sylvia and Josie." She rubbed her arms briskly. "Let me finish with patients and then we can talk more if it's necessary."

"Oh, it's necessary," Laney said. She scrolled through Ana's phone again and started to hand it over when something caught her eye. "Sunday, you said you didn't get the text from your alarm company."

"Correct."

"And Monday night, the broken door didn't sound the alarm, you did."

"From the garage, yes," Ana confirmed.

"But your windows are wired into the system. That alert should have gone off whether you had the system armed or not."

"I hadn't thought of it."

No. She'd been in shock, Laney remembered. Potentially hours after the attack. She flipped to another page in the folder she'd brought along. "Someone has been running interference."

"How?"

"There's new tech that can mimic a cell tower and cause all kinds of problems. When I look at Sylvia's phone records from the provider, I can see the text messages between her and Nolan that were erased from her phone. In your case, the alert from the security company wasn't erased from your phone. It never got there to begin with."

"That's possible?"

"It isn't easy and it sure isn't cheap." Laney rolled her shoulders. "But it seems to be what happened." She frowned at the information. "Whoever did it had to be close to your phone, between you and the tower in fact."

"Close enough to shoot at my house?"

Laney met her gaze. "To shoot at *you*." When Ana blanched, Laney thought she'd open up and be honest. "I can't solve this, can't protect you if you keep holding back."

"Sylvia's letter explains that everything she knew or we suspected is on the drive. Yolanda is giving her statement to Griff."

"You're going to stand there and tell me that will be enough?" Laney snapped.

"I haven't seen the information on the drive, yet. Once I do, if I have something to add, I'll reach out."

Laney slapped Ana's phone into her hand. "Do I tell you how to treat patients? Would you even let me try?"

"No."

"Then stop trying to do *my* job," she said, at the end of her rope now. "The thing is, Ana, you don't know my work. You don't seem to realize every piece matters in an investigation like this. Hell, the entire town is in crisis, confidence in the police department has never been so low. Without *all* the pieces, I'll never see the whole picture."

Ana set her phone beside the tablet on the counter. She rubbed her temples and when she lifted her face Laney knew she was about to get the truth. *Finally.*

Just as her lips parted, McCabe burst into the room. "We need to get back and reevaluate the case."

Laney saw Ana, on the verge of opening up, close down again. She looked at the doctor. "We are *not* done."

McCabe gave her a long questioning look and she ignored him. Gathering the documents she'd brought with her, she followed the chief out of the room, out of the clinic.

Back at the station, she listened to his rundown on the conversation with Yolanda. The woman's suspicions about her husband were damning indeed.

"Any follow up questions?" McCabe asked.

Laney shook her head. "You know them better than I do. It was smart for you to handle it." She reached back and tightened her ponytail, thinking through the case from the moment Renata had found Sylvia's body.

"With that stack of cash in the safe, we know more than a few people had motive to want Sylvia dead," she said. "Though we may never know how many."

"We also know from the coroner that a man taller and far stronger than her and likely known to her is the killer. Zion fits that description."

"Known to her," Laney echoed, laying out the pictures, turning them. "And nothing new or helpful, despite Zion's insane reward."

"You're thinking the reward was a red herring."

Was she? "The reward would keep him involved with the investigation. He'd know if there were witnesses. Know what to do to mitigate any damage." She rubbed at the tension between her brows. "Does it work for you?" she asked. "Zion killing his daughter?"

McCabe let loose a soft whistle. "Yolanda believes it, even without solid proof. We owe it to her to find out one way or another. What did you find on Ana's cell phone?"

She cocked an eyebrow at the first-name familiarity and let it pass. "Not the same trouble we found with Sylvia's phone. Someone cleared the activity from Sylvia's phone. In Ana's situation, it looks more like someone diverted the signal."

"Which leaves us where?"

Laney pulled out the little unicorn flash drive and letter, setting both on the desk. "With more work to do."

McCabe poked at the unicorn without picking it up. "Where'd this come from?"

"Ana said she got this flash drive and the letter earlier today. Apparently Sylvia left both items for her at Duval's place."

He scowled at the unicorn as he reached for the letter. Reading it, his scowl deepened. "He took Josie." McCabe swore. "I wish this was enough." He flicked the paper. "We need to look into this Sergio Rojas before we bring in Zion to ask about the day Josie went missing."

"Definitely." She tipped her head toward his computer. "I'm thinking the tech that interfered with Ana has to be in a car. We'd need a warrant."

"All right." McCabe plugged the flash drive into his computer. "The letter might get us started, but let's see what the unicorn has to say. Has Ana looked at it?"

"She claims she hasn't had a chance," Laney replied. "She read the letter and tried to get into Zion's office for the recording device, but she says it was locked. I think she knows the name in that letter," she added.

"What makes you say that?"

Laney patted her stomach. "Intuition."

"Holy crap." McCabe leaned closer to the monitor. "These are Zion's credit card records and bank statements."

Laney came around the desk, reading over his shoulder as McCabe opened each file and paged through the information. She tapped his shoulder and pointed to a large purchase. "What's that?"

He clicked to enlarge the details on the transaction. "Purchase at a tech company."

"At that price point it just about has to be the cell tower mimic." Laney could feel the net drifting down over Zion Cole. "How much credence do we give Sylvia's comment about hiding Josie on the old homestead?"

"One step at a time, deputy chief." McCabe took a screen shot of the transaction and continued searching.

She pointed to another folder and he clicked to open it. "That's a file on the Windermeres. Good grief. Open it." She skimmed the connections Sylvia had been trying to make between the host family and the missing girls. "Glad we cleared them before she exposed a hell of a mess."

"Look at this." McCabe clicked the mouse to open another folder. It was a collection of articles and screen shots about missing teenage girls. Two from Josie's old neighborhood in Venezuela, per the notes. The reports and research went back, missing teens from every neighborhood that had sent an exchange student to Shutter Lake.

"No wonder they suspected the Windermeres, especially after she discovered Quentin's previous side hustle," Laney said.

McCabe grumbled an agreement. "We could've used her on the police force," he said.

Laney moved back to the files littering the desktop. Finding the print out of Sylvia's cell phone records, she paged back to the day Josie supposedly returned to Venezuela. Again, data from Sylvia's phone didn't match with the provider's record. She pointed out the discrepancy to McCabe.

Piece by piece, she thought. "Zion has to be suspicious. He'll harass Ana about being locked away from Yolanda."

McCabe sat back in his chair. "Afraid Zion will make a move on either his wife or the doc?"

"We'd be fools to think otherwise."

"You're smart as a whip," McCabe said. "I may be a recovering drunk, but I'm no fool."

"Recovering?" The sideways declaration was great news, barely suppressing her excitement. He wouldn't want her making a scene about it. His eyes were clearer, she realized and his mind sharp, though she knew he still felt out of his depth with this investigation. "When was your last drink?"

"Sunday night." He hitched a shoulder. "Still practicing the sobriety thing."

"You'll get there," she said. It gave her a burst of confidence for the department and the town. Assuming they could give the residents closure by solving this case. "I'm behind you all the way."

McCabe grunted.

"We could bring him in, question him," she suggested, shifting back to the matter at hand.

"He'll bluster and lawyer up before we can get him into the interrogation room."

"And the city council will come calling too." Laney swore under her breath. "What if we set a trap?"

"Give him enough rope to hang himself?"

"Stranger things have happened. We could stroke his ego." She snapped her fingers. "Or let him know we have a claim on the reward. A witness who identified someone else."

"Someone else…" He spread his hands. "Like who?"

"What about the missing credit cards and cash?"

We could say one of the cards was used out near San Francisco."

McCabe shook his head. "Not a chance. Assuming Zion has the cards he'll know it's a lie."

"Well then how do you want to get him in here?" she asked.

"Josie."

Laney propped her hands on her hips. "What about her?"

"Quentin saw her through airport security," McCabe said. "We know she didn't get on the plane, thanks to Julia and her FBI pal. Which means she had to have received a message from someone she trusted to leave the airport before boarding."

"Right! I'll go back through the phone records. Zion must have used Sylvia's phone and erased the message. He was always dropping by the Sparkle office. Access to his daughter's phone would have been a piece of cake."

"I'll set up security for Yolanda at the clinic and then start picking apart this Rojas guy Sylvia mentions."

"That Rojas name was also on the short list Ana gave us," Laney said.

McCabe cocked an eyebrow. "Well, I doubt that's a coincidence."

Plan set, they got to work.

CHAPTER SIXTEEN

Ana was often ready for the day to be over, but this one couldn't end soon enough. An hour past closing they were finally locking the front doors and turning the reception phone to the answering service. Donovan was taking the overnight shift and one of the staff nurses agreed to sit with Yolanda through the dinner hour, having been part of Sylvia's circle of friends in high school.

Renata and Lucy were just walking in the back door to handle the general cleaning as Ana headed to her office. She said hello, made sure they were doing okay after the long emotional day, and told them not to worry about tending to her office.

As the three of them went their separate ways, she deliberately ignored the notion that the exchange might be her final farewell to two hardworking, lovely women.

She'd barely settled behind her desk when Griff called with an update that Officer Delaney would be posted at the clinic as extra security until he and Laney could get there.

"I'm picking up dinner for all of us from Stacked in about an hour," Griff said. "What would you like me to bring over?"

She knew better than to argue with him. "The Wednesday special is fine." The roasted turkey with bacon, lettuce, tomato, avocado, and honey mustard was his favorite. If she wasn't going to eat, the least she could do was make sure Griff would enjoy the leftovers.

She was down to her final hours in the community she loved so much. She'd much rather spend that time watching the sunset over the lake than closed up in her office.

She didn't like lying to Griff, but it couldn't be helped. She finally understood what she had to do. Her best chance of catching Zion and putting him out of the trafficking business meant exposing herself.

Her identity and career was a small price to pay in the grand scheme of things.

She logged into the cloud account where she'd copied and stored the information from the drive Sylvia had left behind. Slowly, she picked through the files documenting teenagers who'd gone missing most recently.

Choosing three particular cases, she looked at the dates and banking records Sylvia had gathered. Her intention was only to give the forensic teams a head start. She was sure she could narrow down the transfers from Zion to her father and vice versa.

The further she'd run from her father, the more she understood exactly how effective he was at keeping his nasty operation going. It was terrifying to know her father's business had survived this long, generally unchecked. As she worked, adding to and organizing a formal report for Laney and Griff, she found a poetic justice in two powerful, vile men being taken down by the daughters they didn't value.

Sylvia knew enough of her father's business habits to have pinpointed the financial transactions that coincided with missing teenagers. Ana knew how her father operated and moved the girls from acquisition to jobs to auctions. Though it would take more tracking, she wrote up the likely choke points at various borders and ports for authorities to dig into.

She couldn't believe he was using the same import/export company, but it all fit when she checked the company's public records at the port nearest Colombia. Her father believed hiding in plain sight and generous bribes were the most secure and profitable business model.

It was hard to argue with his success.

He'd always kept business level and the cash flowing with legitimate transports, but she remembered his patterns well enough to put the SLPD and hopefully the FBI on the right track.

Ana looked through the rest of the files before making the call that would change everything.

When the person on the other end answered, Ana felt her world shift. During her ER rotation in Texas she'd met a young undercover officer working to break a trafficking ring. Ana had given her a pattern to look for and the names of her father's top lieutenants.

The officer had used the information and made the bust. She'd returned to the hospital weeks later and asked Ana for an extended interview. Though Ana couldn't give her all she'd hoped for at the time, they had stayed in touch until Ana had accepted the Shutter Lake position and believed she'd left those horrors behind.

In Spanish she delivered the tip to her old friend.

Checking the clock she realized it was past time to go if she wanted any kind of head start. Locking her office door, she pulled the tote she always kept packed from the back of her closet. Quickly, she slipped out of her dress and heels and into jeans, a long-sleeved tee and a heavy sweater. She tugged warm socks over her feet and laced up her hiking boots, determined to be prepared for anything.

Ana quietly left the clinic and drove out of town, down Old Mine Road. She pulled to a stop on the far side of the bridge where it wouldn't be so easy to spot her car. The pieces Laney and Griff had now would probably be enough to convict Zion, but if she could find the place he kept Josie before he'd tossed her in the river, that would be the real coup.

He'd practically dumped Josie's body in his own backyard. The arrogance of it offended her as much as the abuse and crime itself.

Guilt swamped her.

The girl had undoubtedly suffered. Nearby. Ana closed her eyes as the faces of others who'd endured humiliation and abuse at her father's hand paraded through her mind. Her attempts to help them then had failed. Here, watching the river flow under the bridge, she knew she could do something more.

Men like Zion Cole wore two faces, one respectable and one hideous. Being a respected pillar of the community would only make his despicable actions more unbelievable. If she had an escape hatch, she was sure Zion did too. Money and power only made it easier to hide the crimes.

He'd gotten to know Josie and then he'd isolated her so he could kidnap her. Ana knew the system. He must have held her somewhere nearby. Somewhere within easy driving distance, she thought, recalling Yolanda's comments about his driving habits.

No, she didn't have proof, only intuition and firsthand experience watching her father operate. She thought of the letter and wondered if Zion had been dumb enough to keep Josie on his property.

It would have been an arrogant move which fit Zion to a tee.

Ready to explore, she took the back roads out of town and across to the north side of the Cole property. In the waning light, it was difficult to see, but she found the service road that was little more than a dirt track. She went as far as the overgrowth would allow in her car and then parked and pocketed the key.

Grabbing her flashlight, phone, and a bottle of water, she hiked down the trail Sylvia had shown her a couple years ago. About a half mile in she found the clearing. What had once been a service shed now had windows and a door with a padlock on the front. At the peak of the plywood roof, she saw a small satellite dish and an antenna.

She picked her way around the dilapidated structure, looking for more evidence that someone had been here recently. Of course, that didn't necessarily mean it had been Zion with Josie, but it upped the odds.

After pausing to listen for any activity inside, she stepped to the window and shined her flashlight through the glass pane. A short chain, maybe six or eight feet long, was looped around a corner support post and bolted in. At the other end, open on the floor was an adjustable wrist cuff like her father had used.

Damn it. Her gut clenched and roiled.

"What do you think of the accommodations?"

She whirled around and raised her flashlight to Zion's face, ashamed she'd allowed him to sneak up on her. "You kept her here."

He held up a hand to cut the glare of the light, but he advanced on her with a confident stride. "I've kept them all here. And you'll be next."

She let him come closer. Her best option to escape was his certainty of success. A man of his stature frequently underestimated those he didn't find worthy. She swung the flashlight at his head, but he'd anticipated the move and dodged it.

He rushed her, clutching her throat and pinning her to the rough wall of the shed.

"Your father will be so happy I've found you. It's high time you took your *rightful* place in our operation."

She couldn't speak with his hand crushing her windpipe. Gripping his arm, she scratched, hoping to leave some trace of the encounter on him, or her. He shook her, hard, and she managed to land a kick to his weak knee. It was enough to loosen his hold and she clawed his hand as she dropped to her knees and scooted around the corner of the shed.

"You bitch!" he shouted after her. "Come now, Sofia." He said the three syllables of her name a taunting sing-song and she sobbed.

"Yes, yes, I know your secrets. There's nowhere you can go that we won't find you. No one can stop us. Not even the illustrious FBI."

She scrambled to the front of the shed and pulled out her phone. She couldn't hope to make it back to her car, but maybe she could lead someone here. She called the clinic and left the line open.

"Sofia," he said again. "You can't escape. Rojas put a bounty on your head when I told him you were alive, where you lived."

She bolted for the trees. Losing him in the dark was her only hope. A heavy mass landed on her legs, slammed her down to the ground. She scooped up a handful of dirt and debris and threw it as his face before he could get his hands around her neck.

He swore and she twisted away. He caught her ankle, dragged

her back. Her hand found a branch and she swung hard at his head. With the size and reach advantage, he blocked this blow too, snatching the branch from her grasp and driving it into her chest.

She couldn't breathe, could only listen as he lectured her.

"You had a place laid out for you and you resisted," Zion said. "You were never meant to be in service for long. Only enough time to understand what was required. Rojas wanted to leave his legacy to you."

The sickening truth of it had her wishing death would come quickly. Her vision was fading, but his voice persisted, tormenting her.

"Imagine my delight to find you, to give my long-time partner a gift like no other. Resolution at last." With one hand still on her neck, he shoved his thumb into the wound on her hand. "You could say it was like removing a splinter."

She jerked under his vicious grip, tried to spit in his face.

He only squeezed her sides with his knees as he continued to strangle her. "Sylvia fought me. Agent Adler fought me. But I always win."

"Let her go, Cole."

Ana was sure the oxygen deprivation was causing hallucinations. That sounded like Griff's voice and a light illuminated Zion's twisted features. She tried to flail and kick, but her body didn't cooperate.

"Let her go, or I shoot," Griff said.

A gunshot echoed a moment later and Zion was screaming, clutching his shoulder. Ana was able to buck him off and the beam of light showed blood blooming across his shirt.

"Shut up," Laney said. "It's a shoulder wound. They heal. Eventually."

Zion screamed again, protesting violently as Griff slapped cuffs on him.

"This is where you held Josie?" he asked. "Adler too?"

"I don't know what you're talking about," Zion replied. "This is private property, I was subduing a trespasser."

"You're scum," Laney said, lunging for him. She searched his pockets and found the key to the padlock on the door.

When she opened it and walked in, she swore. "This is the place all right. There's a camera in the corner and a blanket." She held out something shiny. "Even this."

Seeing the silver poodle pin Sylvia had given to Josie, Ana started to cry and swear and call Zion all sorts of names in Spanish.

Laney held her back when she would have attacked the man and she sobbed on her friend's shoulder while Griff read Zion his rights.

The four of them trudged back up the trail to the turnoff where Griff's Bronco and Laney's car were parked behind Ana's car. It pleased her more than it should to see Zion limping and bleeding.

"It's over," Laney said, picking leaves from Ana's hair. "We heard everything. Lawyers can't get him out of this. I imagine his associates will soon be in custody as well."

Ana walked toward her car, her entire body throbbing and sore as Griff shoved Zion roughly into the back seat of his old Bronco and backed down the rutted track to the road.

"Officer Trask said a call came in from an associate of yours. I didn't have time to chat with her, but she told him she's coming into town for interviews and to help us piece together the data Sylvia gathered. It'll be a day or two."

"Good." Ana wouldn't be here, but Laney could handle it. "You'll like her."

Laney smoothed back her mussed ponytail, watching Griff turn onto the paved road. "That egotistical deviant asked me once if I'd recognize a monster when I saw one. I sure wish I had."

Ana opened her car door, grateful for the interior light to hold back the encroaching darkness. "Hard to recognize a monster wearing such a perfect mask," she said. She hated having that in common with him, but the mask she wore, the persona that kept everyone at arms' length, had been the only way to remake her life and make a difference in the world.

"True," Laney allowed. She used her key fob to turn on her headlights. "At least he's done now."

"It is." Ana's chest ached, less from the brutal fight and more from the soul-deep turmoil. "This end of the operation is closed." She sighed, wishing she could be there to help Yolanda through the tough weeks ahead. "Yolanda is safe and I'm sure the authorities will be able to raid and rescue other victims."

Laney pulled her into a hug. "I'm glad you're safe too."

"How did you find me out here?" Ana wondered when she slipped out of the embrace.

"I put a GPS tracker on your car Tuesday." She circled her finger in the air. "I've seen the 'about to run' face before. I just expected *you* to bolt before you came to the station."

A deep sadness pressed in on Ana from all sides. It would hurt to leave Laney and her other friends, but she couldn't possibly stay. "Tell Dana and Julia I'm sorry," she said.

"Tell them yourself," Laney countered. "We'll have a girls' night at my place tonight. After Keller checks you out."

"I-I can't do that. You know I have to leave."

"No, I don't know any such thing," Laney folded her arms over her chest, waiting. "Explain it to me."

"It's just better if I go." Misery was a heavy weight on her shoulders. Anything else would be an excuse.

"Better how, Dr. Perez?" Laney stalked toward her. "Shutter Lake needs you. Everyone in town needs to *see* the hero who led the police to Josie and Sylvia's killer. They need to be able to thank you."

"Laney, I'm not—"

Her friend held up a hand, palm out to stop her. "You're Dr. Luciana Camille Perez. I've done the digging and verified the records. Your work is vital to this town and you're a good friend to those you let close." She gave Ana another hug. "No one gets this far without a past, Ana. Don't throw away every good thing you've done in some misplaced effort to pay for your father's crimes. Martyrdom is overrated."

That stung. "I'm not a martyr."

"Prove it. Stay. Stand tall. Your friends will support you."

"You heard." Tears clogged her throat, blurred her vision. "You heard what Zion said. You and Griff."

"Griff and I heard the ravings of a murderer and a delusional, power-hungry bastard."

"You can just overlook… everything before I came here?"

"You became a citizen and a good one," Laney said. "That's what counts."

Ana wiped her face on her sleeve. She wasn't used to trusting this much.

"Besides you're a doctor *and* you're rich," Laney continued, grinning. "Almost as rich as the Shutter Lake founders."

"What does that mean?"

"The reward will go to you. What amount did Zion finally settle on?"

"I'm not sure," Ana replied.

"Well you can bet Yolanda will know." Laney's laughter carried out over the mountains. "That's justice. And Quentin added a million to it. The smart money says they'll both happily pay you for leading us to the killer."

"You're serious."

Laney slung her arm around Ana's shoulders. "I am. Your secret is safe with me, Ana. But I believe your secret would be safe with Julia and Dana too. If nothing else, you should know we'll stick by you. We always have."

"You mean it."

"Come home," Laney spread her hands wide. "We both know you could run the rest of your life and not find a place as beautiful as Shutter Lake or a community as devoted to your weekly yoga classes."

Ana laughed, amazed by the sudden lightness in her heart. Laney was right. Now that the monster had been cleared out, the community would need faces they knew to rebuild trust and connection.

Home. It was a wonderful concept. Almost as wonderful as having a friend who knew her secrets and accepted her anyway.

EPILOGUE

Saturday, October 27

"Trick or Treat!"

Goblins, clowns, fairy queens and everything in between were running amok through the town square for the school's annual Fall Carnival. A young boy dressed up in a fuzzy moose costume dashed by Ana, the wide antlers tilting at an odd angle and the bright orange bucket in his hand nearly full of candy.

The moose's father chased after him. "Happy Halloween, Dr. Perez!"

She returned the sentiment with a laugh, enjoying the freedom of such a happy sound.

This was just the prelude. In a few days these same children would dress up again and descend on their neighborhood streets for the real haul of sugar and treats. This year, even her staff was getting in on the action with a not-so-scary maze built by the school drama club connecting candy stops at the Chamber of Commerce and the clinic.

On her way to the Wine and Cheese House to meet Laney, Dana, and Julia for a girls' night, she paused to watch Griff at the dunk tank. After a bit of taunting and trash talk, the star pitcher on the baseball team threw a strike and Griff splashed into the water to a chorus of good-natured cheers.

In ten short days, it seemed Shutter Lake had righted itself.

It made sense. Zion Cole, the local wolf in sheep's clothing, was in custody and being held without bail for the murders of both Sylvia and Josie. Ana's throat had healed and she could almost make it through a day without recalling the pressure of his hands around her neck.

"Come on, doc." Laney caught up with her, slipped her arm through Ana's. "You can drop off new cold medicine for him tomorrow. Tonight's for friends. Dana's probably wondering what's taking us so long."

It was hard to imagine Dana slipping away to their gathering before the carnival wound down and the last tiny ghost escorted home. Then again, she'd been working overtime this past week fine-tuning the details so everything went perfectly. "She's probably already ordered the stuffed mushrooms," Ana said.

Laney grinned. "Let's find out."

Walking down the block to the restaurant, Ana was tempted to thank Laney once more for rescuing her from Zion's murderous intentions. She'd done her job out in the woods, but more, she'd convinced Ana that though they'd been on a rocky patch, they were still friends.

It was a remarkable feeling.

"Don't." Laney cut her off, opening the front door as they reached the restaurant.

"Don't what?" Ana asked.

"Thank me." Laney rolled her eyes. "You get a look on your face," she explained. "Plus, it's my job to read people. How long until you accept that I'm a fixture in your life? Do we need to pinky swear?"

"Funny." Still, Ana felt a smile curving her lips. "Do you still have a GPS tracker on my car?"

"That's for me to know," Laney joked.

At the table, Julia shifted to make room for Ana and Dana did the same for Laney

"Mushrooms are on the way," Dana said. "Mozzarella sticks too. I don't know what the rest of you are having. This principal needs a carb booster shot," she said to Ana.

"Smart treatment approach," Ana said. "Better if you share."

"I ordered a bottle of red," Julia said. "And an extra sampler platter for the rest of us to start with. Dana isn't the only one who needs fortification." She aimed a severe look at Dana. "You conned me when you said the ring toss would be an easy station."

Overtired, Dana started to giggle.

"Hold off on that red." Laney caught their server's eye. "I have something better."

The server brought over a chilled bottle of champagne and four narrow flutes. Ana's heart gave a happy kick when the cork popped and the bubbly, golden liquid foamed into each of the glasses.

"You have news." Ana sat forward.

Laney waited until the server was out of earshot. "First, to Sylvia, for standing up to her father and fighting for Josie and all the other victims of Zion Cole."

They each touched glasses, the crystal ringing brightly, and sipped in the soft silence that followed.

"Tell them," Julia said.

Ana glanced at Dana, but she only shrugged. Laney's smile was pure satisfaction.

"Yolanda did it," Laney began. She waited out the small swell of triumph around the table. "We all knew Zion wouldn't talk, but Yolanda knows their land as well as, if not better than, him. She found Agent Adler's grave."

Ana sucked in a breath as relief washed over her.

"I've already told Rick," Julia said, clearly as pleased as Laney. "He'll be here tomorrow to escort Adler's remains back to his family."

"Cole never expected us to find the body, so I'm confident we'll find something on the remains to tie him to the crime."

Ana raised her glass. "To Yolanda. I'm not sure I've met a stronger woman. She finished what her daughter started." Once more they touched glasses and sipped.

"I don't know." Dana held up her glass and caught the gaze of each of them in turn. "There are four remarkably resilient women right here at this table. To us! May we never forget the priceless gift of friendship that celebrates and endures through all of life's seasons."

Ana's heart was full to bursting. Leave it to Dana to know just what they all needed to hear. The food arrived and as the server refilled their champagne she realized this was the first girls' night out that she felt complete and whole and wholly accepted for the woman she'd become.

True friends and the hope they offered were the perfect antidote to tragedy of any kind.

THE BREAKDOWN NOVELS

DON'T MISS

If you enjoyed **what she knew**, please consider leaving a review so other readers can find the book too. Review

Read Ana's short story, **trust no one**, for a glimpse at the event that pushed her toward her career in Shutter Lake. You can find this story at Regan Black's website, or grab a Kindle copy now at Amazon.

The BREAKDOWN Novels (best read in order)
the dead girl by Debra Webb
so many secrets by Vicki Hinze
all the lies by Peggy Webb
what she knew by Regan Black

THE BREAKDOWN SHORT READS

In every life there is a defining moment. Take a deep look back into the lives of Laney, Dana, Julia, and Ana with these four short reads about the critical moments that pushed each of them toward a fresh start in Shutter Lake.

Read Laney's story: ***no looking back*** by Debra Webb
Read Dana's story: ***her deepest fear*** by Vicki Hinze
Read Julia's story: ***just one look*** by Peggy Webb
Read Ana's story: ***trust no one*** by Regan Black

ABOUT THE AUTHOR

Regan Black, a USA Today bestselling author, writes award-winning, action-packed romances featuring kick-butt heroines and the sexy heroes who fall in love with them. Raised in the Midwest and California, she and her family, along with their adopted greyhound and two arrogant cats now reside in the South Carolina Lowcountry where the rich blend of legend, romance, and history fuels her imagination.

For early access to new releases, exclusive prizes, and much more, subscribe to the monthly newsletter at ReganBlack.com/perks.

Keep up with Regan online:
www.ReganBlack.com
Facebook
Twitter
Instagram

ALSO BY REGAN BLACK

Unknown Identities Series

Bulletproof

Double Vision

Sandman

Death-Trap Date

Unknown Identities - Brotherhood Protectors crossover novellas:

Moving Target | Lost Signal | Off The Radar

Escape Club Heroes Romantic Suspense

Escape Club, prequel

Safe In His Sight | A Stranger She Can Trust

Escape Club: Justice, novella

Escape Club: Sabotage, novella

Protecting Her Secret Son | Braving The Heat

More Romantic Suspense

Killer Colton Christmas | Colton P.I. Protector

Runaway Secret

Romantic Suspense written with Debra Webb

Against The Wall

Too Far Gone

Nothing to Lose

The Hunk Next Door | Heart of a Hero |

To Honor and To Protect

Her Undercover Defender | Gunning For The Groom | Heavy-Artillery Husband | Investigating Christmas | Marriage Confidential | Reluctant Hero

For a full list of Regan's books visit ReganBlack.com

Subscribe to Regan's newsletter and never miss a new release!

Made in the USA
Monee, IL
20 February 2020